PU
SUMMER

The night he is brough
lonely and miserable as
and aunt are sympath.......... he responds with an
increasing interest in their farm and the surrounding
countryside. Soon he is able to do a full day's work on
the farm, which he loves. But his happiest moments are
those spent with old Ben Huggett, who teaches him the
many secrets of the countryside. At last Dan has found
something he is good at, a world in which he feels
completely at ease, and his having to return home is only
bearable because he knows that one day he will be back
and that the farm, and his many new friends, will be
waiting for him.

Brigid Chard was married to a schoolmaster and had
four daughters. She died in 1982. *Summer for a Lifetime*,
first published in 1975, was her first novel.

SUMMER FOR A LIFETIME

Brigid Chard

ILLUSTRATED BY
TERRY RILEY

PUFFIN BOOKS

PUFFIN BOOKS

Published by the Penguin Group
27 Wrights Lane, London w8 5tz, England
Viking Penguin Inc., 40 West 23rd Street, New York, New York 10010, USA
Penguin Books Australia Ltd, Ringwood, Victoria, Australia
Penguin Books Canada Ltd, 2801 John Street, Markham, Ontario, Canada l3r 1b4
Penguin Books (NZ) Ltd, 182–190 Wairau Road, Auckland 10, New Zealand
Penguin Books Ltd, Registered Offices: Harmondsworth, Middlesex, England

First published under the title *Ferret Summer* by Rex Collings Ltd 1975
Published in Puffin Books 1990

Text copyright © Rex Collings Ltd, 1975
Illustrations copyright © Terry Riley, 1990
All rights reserved

1 3 5 7 9 10 8 6 4 2

Made and printed in Great Britain by
Richard Clay Ltd, Bungay, Suffolk
Filmset in 10/12½ Monophoto Baskerville

Except in the United States of America,
this book is sold subject to the condition
that it shall not, by way of trade or otherwise,
be lent, re-sold, hired out, or otherwise circulated
without the publisher's prior consent in any form of
binding or cover other than that in which it is
published and without a similar condition
including this condition being imposed
on the subsequent purchaser

To Marjorie Groves, my mother

Chapter 1

AFTER THE first two weeks he began to feel better. He liked his Auntie Pat, and it was surprising the way she seemed to know just what he wanted when she had not got any children of her own. Everybody else he knew had children if they were married. He had two older brothers himself, and he wondered sometimes why Uncle Jim and Auntie Pat had not got a family. Once he had asked his mother but all she had said was that it was a great tragedy, which did not explain anything. He did not see how it could possibly be a tragedy when, according to his mother, children meant lots of washing, and money for new shoes and clothes, and trying to make ends meet and not being able to go out with Dad because they could not get babysitters.

Auntie Pat did not have to worry about anything like that, or nag about bouncing on the furniture, or mud on the carpets, or tidying things away before you went to bed. Actually he had a shrewd suspicion she would not have nagged anyway. She bought him a pair of gumboots on his first day, and showed him the bench in the porch where he was to leave them when he came inside, but that wasn't nagging. Uncle Jim and George the cowman both wore gumboots and took them off in the porch, so of course she expected him to do it as well. He was secretly rather proud of the sight of his small pair of boots next to the two pairs of big ones, lined up neatly upon the bench. It made him feel he really belonged, especially when they did not look new any longer.

Inside, the house was so comfortably untidy that no one seemed to notice if he left things lying about. The porch led straight into the kitchen, which was lovely because he could smell things cooking while he was still outside and could try guessing what was for dinner. There was a big wooden table, and wooden chairs with curved, carved backs, much nicer than the shelf thing and stools in the kitchen at home. All the plates and cups were kept on a dresser against the wall, and they were all different colours and patterns, with envelopes and pieces of string and old stamp books and things tucked in behind them, so he never knew what he would find when he laid the table.

Auntie Pat cooked on a big black stove, with a proper fire in it, not electric, and her pots and pans were black too, and very heavy. The stove was always warm, and there was a rocking chair next to it with a patchwork cushion, and a very faded rug made of lots of different coloured rags. There were geraniums on the window-sill above the big stone sink, and the cat usually sat there as well, so he had to be careful not to splash her when he washed his hands.

Next to the kitchen was the living-room which had great big flowery armchairs, a coal fire and lots of books. There were piles of magazines too, funny ones he had never seen before, with pictures of cows instead of ladies, and articles about fertilizers and dairy herds.

Upstairs he had his own bedroom with a little window that stuck out of the roof, and a funny shaped ceiling. He liked waking up in the morning and lying quietly, listening to the sparrows chattering on the slates outside. They were more peaceful than his brothers Tony and John, who were so full of energy they seemed to attack each day as soon as it arrived. It was nice too, he found after the first few days, to wake up feeling almost well again, so that he looked forward to each day, and was really quite hungry enough to be pleased when he heard Auntie Pat shout,

'Dan, Dan, breakfast's ready. Come down and get it and wash afterwards.'

But he had been miserable to begin with, though he hoped Auntie Pat had not noticed as he did not want to upset her. He seemed to have upset everyone recently. Dad had taken a day off to bring him as Mummy did not like driving all that way, and the journey had been horrid. He had not been out of hospital long and the car made him feel sick, like going to a party when you don't want to go, and when they arrived his knees went wobbly and he wanted to cry. They had tea, which he could not eat, and then Dad had said, 'Run along and have a look round outside.'

'Oh Geoff, it's quite chilly out, and he must be awfully tired,' Auntie Pat had protested, but Dad had just frowned at her.

'Do as you're told, Dan, and run along,' he said. 'It'll do you good after being in the car all day.'

So he had zipped himself into his anorak and gone, because he knew it was just an excuse to get him out of the way so they could talk about him. He supposed Dad was telling them about everything, and he wished they didn't have to know.

There was a stone water trough on the far side of the yard, so he wandered over to it, and found a piece of stick to float. He pushed it to and fro in the water, so that it would look as if he was playing if anyone was watching. He felt shut out and very unhappy, and there was so much he did not understand.

The most important thing was simple enough. He'd failed the entrance exam to the school where his twin brothers had gone. They were four years older than him, and very clever. They were going to be doctors. Dad had explained to him ages ago that that meant he had to get into the same school, too, so that he could be a solicitor like Dad and keep the family firm going. He quite liked the idea of being a solicitor. He wasn't sure what a solicitor did, but he liked the office with its piles of papers, and big dusty books, and the atmosphere of quiet bustle.

So he had worked very hard, partly for Dad, and partly because it was the only way to get the better of the boys at school who teased him because he wasn't good at football, and didn't like fighting in the playground. But as the date of the exam drew nearer he got more and more nervous, and the grown-ups made it worse by telling him to work hard and saying how important it was.

'Your whole future depends on it,' Dad had said, and he had tried, he really had; but even so he had failed.

He thought he would never forget the morning the letter had come. Dad had been so grim and quiet, and Mummy had cried, and he had had such an awful pain in his tummy and had not dared to tell them. So he had gone to school as usual; and he had to tell everyone that he had failed. And the other boys had laughed at him because now they knew he was no good at anything.

The rest of the day was muddled, all mixed up with pain, and being sick, and the hospital. He had been very ill; appendix, they said. When at last he came home he had wanted to tell them how sorry he was, but they would not listen. They said it did not matter but he knew it did. He was a disappointment, he had let them down, and there was nothing he could do about it now. He had done his best, but it had not been good enough. All Dad's plans were ruined.

He sniffed, and rubbed the tears off his cheeks with the back of his hand. It was sissy to cry and he seemed to cry so often now. His stick had grown waterlogged, and was sinking, and he was wondering what to do next when the yard gate clicked, and he saw George coming towards him.

He had come on day visits to the farm before with the rest of the family, so he knew George, and liked him. He had sandy hair and a red freckled face and his big squared hands were freckled too. He helped Uncle Jim with the farm, and lived in a cottage down the lane with Mrs George and his two small daughters. He was always very friendly and just seeing him made Dan feel better.

'Hello, Dan, hear you're coming to give us a hand for a week or two,' said George cheerfully. 'Proper poorly, Mrs Knott says you've been. Nasty places, hospitals. What you need is a bit of feeding up, and some country air, by the look of you. Seen the new calf yet?'

Dan shook his head.

'Real beauty she is. Come on and have a look at her, she's in the stall over there.' And he led the way to the cattle sheds across the yard. They discussed the calf, and then went to look at the tractor. George wanted to check the engine over, he said it had played him up something shocking that afternoon; and Dan was very busy, holding spanners and chatting to George when his father came to call him back to the house.

Almost immediately Dad had given him a hug and gone away, leaving him standing unhappily by the kitchen door. That had been awful, but Auntie Pat had not given him much time to think about it, just taken him upstairs to wash while she unpacked his case, and then brought him a mug of hot milk to drink in bed. She had sat on the end of the bed while he drank it, talking to him about the things he could do the next day, and by the time she had kissed him goodnight, and turned out the light, he was so tired that he had gone to sleep before he had a chance to realize that he was lonely.

Chapter 2

THE DAYS were full of sun, and interesting things to do. Quite suddenly this morning Dan had realized that he was no longer lonely, that he did not feel ill, and even his unhappiness about the exam was not too bad because Uncle Jim and Auntie Pat behaved as if nothing was wrong at all. But getting better brought its own problems. There was something he had to find out, so he stayed sitting at the table after lunch until Uncle Jim had gone back to work.

'Auntie Pat,' he said, carefully not looking at her so that she would not realize it was important, 'I really feel quite well now. Will I have to go home soon?'

He did not want to. Home meant school, and the thought of having to walk in through the playground gate as though nothing had changed made him feel sick again. His aunt stopped washing up and came back to the table.

'I'm glad you're feeling better, that's why you're here. And it doesn't mean you have to go home. Having your appendix out is nasty, and the doctor said you needed a long holiday, but you can go home if you want to. Do you?'

He shook his head. 'Not really.'

'Then I should stay. We like having you.' She picked up a pile of plates and went back to the sink. 'That's settled then. So what are you going to do this afternoon?'

Relief bubbled up inside him and he relaxed in his chair, thinking of the various possibilities. Uncle Jim and

George were spreading fertilizer, and he was not allowed on the tractor, so he could not go with them. He had spent the morning visiting the calves and scratching the pigs' backs, and sailing bits of wood in the water trough, so he did not really want to do that again. There was an apple tree in the garden he had his eye on, but climbing still made his tummy hurt, and anyway there was plenty of time now to do that later.

'I'd like to go out,' he said, 'because it's nice and sunny, but I'm not quite sure what to do *when* I'm out.'

Auntie Pat dried her hands, came back to the table and together they considered the problem. He liked the way she always took this sort of thing seriously, sitting with her chin on her hands, and frowning as though she was really thinking about it.

'I think it's time you went exploring,' she said. 'You know your way round the farm very well, and you've been down to the village with me, so why don't you go off on your own and see what else you can discover? You can go anywhere you like in the woods or across the fields provided you shut gates behind you.'

'Can I go by myself?' he asked, astonished. He was not allowed out by himself at home, except to walk to school, or to play with the other children on the estate.

'Oh yes, it wouldn't be proper exploring if you had someone with you. I'll lend you my watch so you know what time it is, and you can take some food as well. You can't get lost if you notice the landmarks and come home the same way. Just see you're back in time to help George bring the cows in.'

A few minutes later, with Auntie Pat's watch strapped to his wrist, a bag of biscuits and an apple stuffed into the pocket of his jeans, and a ten pence piece tied tightly in the corner of his handkerchief, he crossed the yard and went through the gate, carefully shutting it behind him.

14

The lane was narrow, with high hedges. He knew that if he turned left he would come to the village, so he set off to the right, feeling like Livingstone faced with darkest Africa. He had been a little way in this direction before, just as far as George's cottage with a message, but after that it was all unknown. There was the cottage now, with Mrs George taking the washing off the line. She waved to him, and called 'Hallo, Dan, off for a walk?'

'I'm going exploring,' he called back, but did not stop because Mrs George talked a lot, and he did not want to waste time.

Past the cottage the lane twisted so he could not see the farm or Mrs George, and then he really was on his own. The sun was warm, and there were buds on some of the hedge bushes which were beginning to turn into leaves. Most of them were bare though, and he counted five nests in the first ten minutes' walking. He looked inside two of them, but they were empty and rather tattered so he decided they were old ones from last year.

Soon he came to a crossroads, and stopped to decide which way to go. If he went straight on it would be easy to find his way back, but he thought that might be cheating. One road curved back to the left as though it might lead to the village again, and the fourth was not really a road at all but an earthy track with grass growing down the middle.

'That's the one,' he thought, and ran down it very fast so that he could not change his mind.

It led him downhill, patched with sunlight and shadow and very green. The grass at the bottom of the hedge was long and thick, and he pulled a stem of it and sucked it as he walked. It was juicy and snapped when he bit it. The hedges grew closer together until at last he was walking through a tunnel made by the branches and had to bend his head to avoid the thorns on the brambles which hung like creepers on either side. He wondered whether to turn back but he could see sunlight ahead so he struggled on to emerge scratched and rather breathless into an open field.

The path went on across the field, and now he was out of the bushes he could see that they were really part of a wood which edged the field to the left. In the distance he could just see another clump of trees which he thought must be the ones behind the farm. He was rather pleased that he had recognized them because it meant he could go home a different way across the fields and anyway, real explorers always recognize landmarks.

He wandered a little way into the wood, but it was not very exciting so he did not stay long. The dead leaves were still thick on the ground, and there was nothing growing there except dog's mercury, great patches of it, where the light came through the branches. In spite of the sun it was quite muddy underfoot, and near the edge of the wood he found a bare patch with some very odd animal prints showing clearly in the mud. He wished he knew what they were, and spent quite a long time studying them, until he suddenly felt hungry and wandered out again to eat his food. It was nice lying in the warm sun, so he ate three biscuits and then decided to eat his apple too, and was half-way through it when the old man appeared.

Actually, it was the dog he saw first. It came stepping delicately and silently along the edge of the wood, a lovely greyhound-shaped dog, ears pricked and nose close to the ground. Its coat was a curious mixture of black and brown, which made it quite difficult to see against the shadows of the trees, and it was obviously very busy. It was so interested in what it was doing that it was quite close to Dan before it saw him, and then it stood still and growled at him, and the hair rose in a ridge all the way down its spine.

Dan stayed still too, not because he was frightened but

because he thought that the dog was. Then, looking at it out of the corner of his eye, because he knew dogs did not like being stared at, he moved one hand very slowly into the paper bag, and got out a biscuit.

'Hello, dog,' he said quietly. 'I'm sorry if I made you jump. Come on and have a biscuit.'

The dog inched towards him, hackles down but still rumbling a warning. Dan went on talking until at last it was close enough to sniff at his hand. It was pleased with the biscuit and stopped growling, so Dan gave it another one. He stroked its coat, which was short and silky, and it rolled on its back so he could tickle its tummy.

The voice made them both jump.

'Dang me,' it said. 'I never thought I'd see that!'

The dog thumped its tail and sat up, and Dan turned round. Behind them stood an old man. He was tall and thin and grey. His shirt had no collar, his jacket was shapeless and bulged in peculiar places, and his old trousers were tied round below his knees with hairy string. But he had the most beautiful waistcoat Dan had ever seen, made of strips of close black fur, and with six silver buttons.

'Well dang me!' he said again. 'Won't go to anyone but me, that Dog. What've you been doing to him?'

'He liked having his tummy tickled, and he seems rather fond of biscuits. Would you like one too? They're ginger.' Politely Dan offered him the paper bag.

'Don't mind if I do. Reckon I'm as deserving as old Dog here.'

Chuckling, the old man sat down and took the biscuit. He ate it in silence, staring contentedly across the field, and then carefully brushed the crumbs off his waistcoat.

'And where are you from, young man? Haven't seen you before hereabouts.'

'I'm staying with my aunt and uncle at the farm. That

one up there by those trees.' He pointed across the fields
to the right.

'That'll be Mr and Mrs Knott of Willowgarth.'

'That's right.'

'And what are you doing way down here then?' The old
man's eyes were bright with friendly curiosity.

'Oh, Auntie Pat sent me exploring. She thought I ought
to find my way about on my own because . . .'

'Sh!' The man's hand on his arm stopped him. 'Down
there – see? That's a grand sight for a spring day.'

Dan turned his head to look where the old man pointed,
and there stepping out from the wood was the most
beautiful bird he had ever seen. The sun gleamed on its
blue-green head, its back and wings shone like copper, and
its long tail brushed the grass like a prince's cloak. In
silence they watched it strut across the field until it
suddenly saw them, and launched itself into the air with a
whirr of wings.

'Oh.' Dan had been holding his breath. 'What was it? It was beautiful.'

'That's old cock pheasant out looking for his hens. Got his courting coat on, the old dandy. You never seen him before?'

Dan shook his head. 'No, I don't live in the country, you see, so I don't know much about it. I wish I did. It makes me cross when I don't know things. I saw lots of nests today but I couldn't tell who made them, and there are some smashing prints in the wood. I'd love to know what they are.'

The man got to his feet. 'Show me,' he said.

They found the muddy patch easily, and squatted down side by side to look at it. They really were very odd prints, Dan decided; a small blurry mark, then two long thin shapes, and just in front two small round ones joined together.

'Well now, that's not so hard as some.' One brown forefinger touched each mark in turn. 'Let's see if you can guess. This smudge is a tail, and these are back legs, and these front paws. Now, who squats on his back legs with his front paws all nice and neat and his long ears cocked?'

The words made a picture in Dan's mind. 'A rabbit, a rabbit!' he cried excitedly.

'That's right. He stopped here last night to listen and sniff afore he went out into the field. Have to be careful, do rabbits.'

'Two long shapes and two little ones. I'll remember next time I see it.'

They wandered out into the sun again.

'You do know a lot,' said Dan wistfully.

'Ar,' said the old man, and looked at him very hard. His eyes were very bright and his face had the closed look grown-ups get when they are testing you out. Dan felt his stomach sink. The grass and sun faded and he was back in the playground at school with the pointing fingers, and laughing faces, 'Failed, Dan's failed,' and his mother's voice, 'Oh Dan, you've failed, what are we going to do?' His eyes filled with tears and he turned away.

He couldn't believe it when the old man spoke.

'Funny how old Dog took to you. Got sense has old Dog.' He paused. 'Happen I could teach you a thing or two if you really want to learn. I got the time, and I like a bit of company that doesn't natter me. Listen here now. You tell Mrs Knott that you met Ben 'Uggett, and he says you can come down to his place when you've nothing better to do. Reckon that'll make it all right.'

'Oh, Mr 'Uggett,' Dan could hardly speak. 'Oh thank you, thank you *very* much. Please, where is your place?'

'Straight on at the crossroads, and it's the first house you come to. Can't miss it if you keep looking.' He fumbled in his top pocket and drew out a battered watch on a chain. 'Reckon you'd better get back now, or they'll wonder where you got to.'

'Golly, yes, I've got to bring the cows in with Mr George. Will I be late?'

'Not if you go that way, across the field. Tell old George Ben 'Uggett sent his best, and get off with you now.'

'I'll tell him,' said Dan; and then reluctantly, 'I'd better go.'

He shook hands politely, patted Dog and walked away. He could feel Ben Huggett watching him, so he stopped once to wave.

'Come any time then,' Ben Huggett called, and turned down by the wood, moving as quickly and silently as the Dog at his heels.

'Ben 'Uggett,' said Dan to himself. 'Ben 'Uggett.'

Excitement bubbled inside him, and he went leaping and running across the fields to the farm.

Chapter 3

HE WAS out of breath by the time he got to the home meadow where the cows were grazing, and he could feel the familiar sharp pain round the scar on his tummy. It still came when he got tired, and it worried him a bit, so he sat on the top of the gate to get his breath back and rest until it went away. Cows, he decided, were very peaceful. He liked their slow walk, and the way they blew down their noses, and the steady tearing noise they made as they pulled at the grass. Some of them were already moving slowly towards the gate, as though they knew it was milking time, and as he watched the others stopped grazing one by one, until the whole herd was moving in single file across the field as if they were playing a solemn game of follow-my-leader.

'All ready for us, are they?' There was George, calling

as he came down the lane. 'Open the gate and let 'em through, Dan.'

Dan jumped down and swung the gate wide, and the cows plodded through into the lane, filling it with their broad black and white backs. He walked behind them with George, imitating his 'Gerrup there' and 'Gerralong' and occasionally slapping their behinds encouragingly when they stopped to snatch a mouthful of grass.

'George,' he said. 'I was to tell you that Ben 'Uggett sent his best.'

'Did he now,' George looked pleased. 'So you met Ben 'Uggett. Still going strong, is he?'

'He looked very well. He's a nice man, isn't he?'

'One of the best is Ben. Tell some rare tales about him down in the village; and most of them true, I reckon.' George chuckled. 'He was a wild one once, old Ben.'

'What sort of tales, George? Tell me.'

'That I won't.' One big hand reached out to cuff him jokingly on the side of his head. 'Tell you himself if he wants you to know.'

'Oh George . . .'

'Get along with you, there's work to do. Can't keep cows waiting while you gossip. Get that first lot fed, and the neck chains on, while I wash 'em down, so we can start milking.'

They set to work. It was a routine Dan had mastered quickly, and now he moved confidently from stall to stall, tipping the measures of cow cake into the mangers and fastening the chains round each cow's neck so she wouldn't move away when she had finished eating. George washed the cows down, and behind him came Uncle Jim with the strip cup, taking and checking a little milk before he fixed the milking machines to the full udders.

Dan found the whole process very satisfying. He liked the hum of the motor, the steady sucking sound of the machines, the smell of cows and cow cake, and most of all the way he was left to get on with his part of the job on his own. The groups of cows passed through the shed, the milk was carried through to the cooler, the churns filled, and finally everything was hosed down and scrubbed ready for the morning.

'I'll take the cows down and go for me tea then, Mr Knott,' said George, hanging his milking coat on the peg behind the door. 'I'll be back after to finish off that field.'

'Right you are, George, see you later.'

'Cheerio then, Mr Knott; Dan.'

'Cheerio, George,' they said, and 'Come on, Dan,' said Uncle Jim, 'Tea-time, and we've both earned it.'

The table was laid when they went in, and Auntie Pat was taking a pie out of the oven.

'Steak and kidney,' said Uncle Jim sniffing, and she laughed at them both.

'Anyone would think I starved you! Hurry up now before it gets cold. Did you have a good afternoon, Dan?'

'Yes, thank you,' said Dan, scrubbing his hands carefully. 'But I'm very hungry. Can I tell you when I've had my tea?'

He ate his way quickly through his helping of pie, feeling excited and pleased every time he thought of Ben 'Uggett. He wanted to make sure they understood just how extraordinary the afternoon had been, and that the old man really did want to see him again. He watched them as they ate and talked to each other, quiet talk about the farm and the village, his Aunt so quick and bright, explaining things with her hands, her fair hair falling forward to hide her face, and at the end of the table his big dark Uncle, not saying much, just nodding and smiling at her. Everything about Uncle Jim was quiet. He moved unhurriedly about the house and farm, deliberate and slow-speaking, treating animals and people with the same calm gentleness. He never said much, but when he did talk, everyone listened. It was, Dan thought, quite desperately important to explain everything properly to Uncle Jim, and make certain he approved. Would it be better to start at the beginning of the afternoon, or just plunge straight in? He was still trying to make up his mind when Uncle Jim said,

'And what have you been doing, Dan, or is it a secret?'

'Oh no,' said Dan quickly. 'It's not secret, just exciting.' He told them everything; all about Dog, and meeting Ben 'Uggett, and the rabbit prints, and how Ben 'Uggett had said he could come and see him again, and that he would teach him if he wanted to learn. When he had finished Uncle Jim lit his pipe, and thought about it for a while.

'And what do you want to learn about, Dan?' he said eventually, leaning back in his chair.

That was a difficult question. Dan knew the answer but it wasn't easy to put it into words, and he had to get it right. Uncle Jim hardly ever asked questions, and when he did, Dan felt it was only because he really wanted to know.

'Well,' he said slowly, 'When I first came here I didn't know much about the farm at all. We'd only been for the day before, and that was different because we were visitors. But since I've been staying with you, you've let me work with you, and every day I've learnt something new. Sometimes it was something big, like helping with the milking, and sometimes something little, like finding out that pigs like to be scratched. And the more you find out, the more interesting it gets and you begin to understand what people are talking about. And now I don't feel like a visitor any more.'

'That,' said Auntie Pat smiling at him, 'is the nicest thing anyone has said to me for a long time.'

'Well, it's true,' said Dan grinning back. 'Really it is,

and it's smashing when you start to feel you belong. But this afternoon I didn't belong at all. I saw all sorts of things, and I didn't know what they were. If I hadn't met Mr 'Uggett, I couldn't have told you that I saw a pheasant; I'd just have said a funny big bird. Oh, don't you see . . .' His face creased with the effort of trying to make them understand. 'There's so much to find out, and I may never have a chance like this ever again!'

'Dan,' said Uncle Jim firmly, 'if that's the sort of thing you want to learn about, you won't find anyone who can teach you better than Ben Huggett. He's a grand old man, but he's not usually very sociable so he must have taken to you straight away. I can't think of any reason why you shouldn't meet him again. I think you'd be a fool not to. You've my permission to visit him whenever he invites you.'

He put down his pipe and rose, stretching, to his feet.

'Well,' he said. 'I'd better go and help George finish that field before the light goes.' And he kissed the top of Pat's head and went out.

'Oh Auntie Pat! Oh Auntie Pat!' Dan started quietly, but his voice ran away with him, and he ended with a yell of pure joy, and danced round the table. She sat and laughed at him, and when he had sobered down a little said quite seriously,

'I think it's marvellous too, and Jim's quite right you know, I've never known Ben Huggett do anything like this before. You should feel very honoured.'

'Is that what he meant about Mr 'Uggett not being sociable?'

'Yes, it means he's always friendly, but he usually likes to be by himself.'

'I see.' Dan thought about it while they both cleared the table, and then said shyly, 'I think he did like me though. He said he could do with some company that didn't natter him.'

'Oh Dan.' Auntie Pat stopped washing up and gave him a quick hug. 'I can't imagine you nattering anyone. And I'm quite sure he liked you. He's a very wise old man.'

Chapter 4

BEN HUGGETT was digging his garden. It was a Spring ritual which gave him enormous pleasure with each year that he survived to perform it. The Autumn digging was quite different; a kind of tidying up of loose ends, like writing your will, but with the Spring digging he cocked a triumphant snook at Winter, as though he said, You see, I'm still here! I'll make my mark for another year! And there were so many kinds of digging to do in the Spring. There was the gentle podging round the perennials in the flower beds; the soil in the seed beds had to be broken down to a fine tilth, a job the frost had half done for him; and there was the lovely precision of double digging, the spade slicing cleanly into the earth, and the quick flick of the wrist throwing it, dark and gleaming, to the far side of the trench. With so much variety he could choose the one which exactly suited the mood or energy of the moment, and to a man nearing seventy, that is important.

Today he was trenching, ready to plant broad beans, but he wasn't enjoying it as much as usual. If he had known that Pat Knott had called him a wise old man he would have been very scornful. He was feeling far from wise; in fact he thought he'd been plain daft to get himself mixed up with some small boy he'd never set eyes on before. He didn't even like small boys. Nasty noisy creatures, wandering about the place leaving litter everywhere, stealing eggs and breaking branches off the trees. Only the other day some village lads had come up the lane with an

air gun shooting away at everything they saw. When they had gone he had found a dead blackbird they had left lying in the dust at the side of the road, one of a pair which he had fed all winter. The other one was still hanging round the garden, all moithered, with its nest half built, and its mate gone. No manners, too much money, and not enough work to do – that's what was wrong with boys today; so what in Heaven's name had got into him yesterday?

He finished the trench, and stopped, leaning his weight on the spade while he thought about it. The boy was a funny little lad and no mistake, all bones and eyes, no meat on him at all, and he'd seemed quiet enough. Too quiet maybe. And polite too – sharing his biscuits and folding the bag up so nice and neat afterwards. And he'd never seen a pheasant before, poor little begger. He'd felt sorry for him, that's what had done it.

'You're a fool, Ben 'Uggett,' he muttered, driving the

spade firmly into the ground. 'And you're gettin' old, that's what's the matter with you.' And he stomped off up the garden path to fetch a barrow load of compost.

It was good compost this year, well rotted down and helped along by a nice bit of manure George had brought him. He piled it in little steaming heaps by the side of the trench and went for another load.

Dog, lying on the sunny path, eyed it longingly and inched forward, nostrils quivering. The smell was compulsive, waking an instinct from the past which urged him to wallow in it, roll until his own scent was hidden, abandon himself to the bliss of warm decay.

'Get out of it!' yelled Ben, and he collapsed on to the path again, torn between the scent and a memory of harsh words and buckets of cold water. He sighed deeply and rested his head on his forefeet, protest in every line of his body. Ben eyed him warily as he forked the compost into the trench. They fought this particular battle of wills every year, and he had no desire to wash down an evil-smelling and rebellious Dog.

Suddenly Dog sat up, ears pricked. He could hear footsteps, and mingled with the compost was another scent, faint but familiar. His tail thumped on the path as he recognized it, and he trotted towards the gate, stopped and looked inquiringly at Ben.

'Who the Devil's that?' thought Ben, and moved to where he could see over the hedge.

A little way down the lane stood Dan, half turned as though he could not decide whether to go or stay. His hands were deep in his pockets and he was rolling a small stone endlessly to and fro with the toe of one dusty gumboot. He was obviously afraid to come any closer uninvited, and looked so lost that Ben 'Uggett's doubts vanished. Old fool he might be, but he could no more turn the lad away than he could be unkind to Dog.

'Hallo there!' he called.

At the sound of his voice Dan looked up, and then came running. Dog greeted him with abandon, leaping round him, pushing against his legs, and trying desperately to lick his face as Dan bent down to pat him.

'Well, come on in, if he'll let you. Steady now, Dog. Lie down.'

'It's all right, Mr 'Uggett,' Dan wiped his damp face, laughing, 'I like dogs.'

'I can see that,' said Ben dryly. 'You found your way then?'

'Yes, easily,' Dan hesitated. 'Is it all right for me to come today? I'm not disturbing you? Uncle Jim said you were to send me home if I was a nuisance.'

'No, lad, you'll not disturb me.' Ben smiled down at his worried face. 'I'm just planting a row of beans. You can give me a hand if you want.'

'Yes please, I'd love to.' The worry vanished. He would not be in the way if he had a proper job to do, and could actually help Mr 'Uggett. 'Will you show me how to do it, because I've never planted beans before?'

'I'll show you. Wait here with Dog now, and I'll go and get them.'

Dan sat down on the path next to Dog and looked round him, deciding that it was just the sort of place he had imagined Ben 'Uggett living in. The cottage was built on a patch of rising ground between the lane and the end of the wood which he had discovered yesterday, so it was sheltered from the North by the trees, and open to all the sun from the South and West. It was a tiny cottage. From where he sat, Dan could only see five windows, three at the top, and one each side of the front porch, and he thought it must be very old, because the bricks were a soft red, not bright like George's house, and the roof slates had patches of moss growing on them. The garden was surprisingly big. There were two beehives in the far corner, some fruit trees and a large patch which was obviously for vegetables. Where the ground sloped too steeply it had been terraced with little stone walls to hold the soil, and these stepped beds were planted with flowers, the first spring growth already showing so that the different shaped leaves made lovely patterns against the dark earth. Some of them Dan knew, irises and peonies and delphiniums, because he had seen them at home, but most of them he didn't recognize. Quite close to him was a bush already covered with blue flowers, and he could hear the steady hum of the bees as they clustered round it, working busily, as though it were full summer instead of early April. It was a summery sort of garden, Dan thought, with so much sun in it, and yawned lazily.

'Now then, don't go to sleep,' said Ben 'Uggett, and handed Dan a stiff brown paper bag. 'These are the beans, see, and I'll show you what to do with them.'

'Thank you,' said Dan. 'I was listening to the bees. They like that bush, don't they?'

'Rosemary that is, the first flowers of the year. Comes out with the warm days just when the bees start to get busy again. I grow that for them special – got some more round the back. Makes a lovely bit of honey does rosemary. Smell that.' He broke a tiny sprig off, rubbed it between his fingers, and gave it to Dan to sniff. It was a sharp scent, hot and slightly bitter.

'It's nice,' he said.

'Yes, I like a bit of rosemary.' Ben 'Uggett sniffed at it again. 'Our mother always said it smelt like summer. Reckon it does too.' He sighed and stood staring thoughtfully at the rosemary bush.

'Er . . . the beans,' Dan reminded him gently.

Ben 'Uggett chuckled. 'Back to work is it? All right then, beans. Can you play dominoes?'

'Yes,' said Dan, very surprised.

'Right then.' Ben led the way to the trenches he had prepared. 'Now start at the far end and put your beans in so they look like the five on a domino. Space 'em out nice, and when you've done, rake the soil back on top of 'em nice and gentle until they're about an inch under. Can you manage it?'

'I think so.'

'Right you are then, and by the time you've done those, I'll have finished composting this one.'

They worked in silence. When Dan was half-way down the first row Ben came across to look at what he was doing, gave him a nod of approval and a gruff 'That's the way!' and went back to his digging. Proudly and carefully Dan made his domino patterns down the trenches, and then raked the soil over the top to hide them. The sun was warm on his back and it was very peaceful. When they had finished, Ben marked the beginning and end of each row with a stick and they stood and looked at their work with mutual satisfaction.

'There's a good job well done,' said Ben. He fished his watch out of his pocket and looked at it. 'Done quickly too, with the pair of us at it. What do you say to a cup of tea? Reckon we've earned it, don't you?'

He led the way round the corner of the house to the back door. 'Sit you down,' he said pointing to a bench against the wall and disappeared indoors, to return surprisingly quickly with two mugs of strong sweet tea. Ben blew into his mug, sipped, sighed gustily, and set it down beside him to cool.

'Now then,' he said. 'I think it's time we got a bit better acquainted, young man. I don't know your name yet, so let's start with that.'

'Oh,' said Dan. 'How awful. I forgot to tell you! I'm Daniel Hunt, but everyone calls me Dan.'

'Dan it is then.'

'Actually I wish it wasn't. I get awfully teased in school because of it.'

Ben looked puzzled, and then started to chuckle.

'Not that old rhyme?' he said delightedly.

'Dan, Dan the dirty old man.'

'Washed his face in a frying pan,' finished Ben.

'Yes, that's the one,' said Dan bitterly.

'Well I never. We used to sing that when I was a lad. One of my brothers was called Dan – we used to shout it at him just to get him angry. Terrible temper he had.' He chuckled again, remembering. 'Fancy that now; I'd forgotten all about that. And they still sing it at school, do they?'

'Yes, they do. And it's not very nice when it's your name!'

'You don't want to mind them.' Ben laid a comforting hand on Dan's knee. 'The day my brother stopped getting mad, we stopped doing it. Weren't no fun any more. You try it and see.'

Dan thought about it, 'You mean pretend I don't mind, even if I do?'

'That's right. That'll do the trick, you take my word.'

'I'll try it,' said Dan determinedly, 'Thank you very much Mr 'Uggett. I am glad I told you. I've never said anything about it before.'

'Maybe you should a' done,' said Ben wisely, reached for his mug of cooling tea, and drank it thirstily.

'That's better,' he said, putting the empty mug down again, and added; 'Come to that, why aren't you in school now, Dan? 'Tisn't holiday time yet.'

'I've been in hospital, having my appendix out. I'm staying with Auntie Pat until I'm really well again.'

So that was why he looked so thin and poorly, Ben thought, though he had a bit of colour now after an afternoon in the sun. Still he couldn't be very strong.

'Hope I haven't worked you too hard then,' he said.

'Oh no, really you haven't. I've enjoyed it. You've got a lovely garden, Mr 'Uggett. Do you grow all the flowers for the bees?'

'Indeed I don't,' Ben laughed. 'I grew 'em for our mother first. She loved flowers, our mother, and we never had a proper garden when I was a little lad. When we came to live here I said "Now you'll have your flowers, mother," and so she did, all her favourites; hollyhocks and peonies, marigolds, phlox, poppies, honeysuckles, the lot. It's twenty years since she died but I still grow 'em just the same.'

'Golly,' said Dan. Twenty years seemed an awfully long time to keep on growing flowers for someone who wasn't alive any more.

'Your mother must have been very special.'

'She was,' said Ben. 'She was.'

He took Dan round the garden, pleased by the boy's eager interest in showing him his favourite plants, descendants of the ones he had first set all those years ago. Dan particularly liked the herb patch. Ben made him pick a leaf from each one, so he could smell the different scents, strange and bittersweet, like their strange names; southernwood and marjoram; savory and rue; cotton lavender, lemon thyme, tarragon, tansy and many more.

'I'll never remember them,' said Dan.

'You will,' said Ben confidently. 'Funny things, herbs. You have to treat them careful, because they're old plants, and powerful. You can heal with them, or harm with them, but if you like them, they'll grow for you and you'll remember them.' He picked a sprig of southernwood and tucked it into Dan's anorak pocket. 'Take that home and keep it under your pillow. You'll sleep sound and grow strong.'

Dan looked at him wide-eyed. 'Is it magic?' he asked.

34

'No,' Ben smiled. 'Don't you worry, I'm not spelling you. It's not magic, just old-fashioned medicine. I don't hold with doctors meself, and they've left you looking a bit wambly, so you give the old way a try and see if that'll get you right again.'

Dan pushed the southernwood deeper into his pocket. It sounded like magic to him, but if Mr 'Uggett said it would work he was more than ready to trust him.

It was while they were inspecting the honeysuckle which Ben said Mrs 'Uggett had planted herself more than thirty years ago that Dan first noticed the blackbird. The honeysuckle was huge, completely covering a small brick shed some distance from the back door. It was, said Ben, the new 'doings' which the council had made them build. Mrs 'Uggett had objected to the new 'doings'; she thought it spoilt the view, so she had planted the honeysuckle to hide it, which it did most successfully. Puzzled, Dan peered over the half door and saw a narrow wooden platform, like a bench with the front boarded up. There was a hole in the top so he decided it must be a lavatory, and fascinated, wondered what on earth the old 'doings' had been like if this was the new one.

The blackbird flew out of the honeysuckle as they walked towards it, but instead of disappearing into the wood, it stayed quite close, behaving in what Dan thought was a very odd way. Back hunched, wings very slightly spread it huddled under an apple tree. Its beak kept opening and shutting and every now and then it gave a short high-pitched call. Dan tugged at Ben's sleeve.

'Look, Mr 'Uggett, that blackbird. Is it sick? What's the matter with it?'

'There isn't nothing I can do for her, poor girl.' Ben shook his head sadly. 'She'd just started her nest in that honeysuckle when them boys come up from the village with their damn pop guns and shot the old cock bird. She's missing him, and don't know what to do.'

'But what will happen to her?' Dan was horrified.

'She'll get over it soon. It's early yet, there's time for her to pair again.' His voice hardened. 'But if I was ten years younger I'd give those lads what ho! It's the waste I can't abide. Times you've got to kill, for food or to make a living, but there's no call to go killing for the sake of it.' And he looked so fierce Dan felt quite frightened.

The shadows by the hedge were lengthening, and the warmth was going from the sun. Reluctantly Dan decided that it was nearly milking time and he ought to go.

'Run along then,' said Ben. 'But mind you come again.' He smiled with real warmth. 'Don't know when I've known the time pass so quick.'

They walked to the gate together, and he stayed leaning on it, to watch Dan run down the lane. He realized with surprise that he had enjoyed the lad's company, and wondered what he could find to interest him next time he came. He remembered the rabbit tracks, and thought maybe he could take him out into the wood and across the fields. He could show him a thing or two no one else knew about, and it would make a change to have someone to talk to. Perhaps he wasn't such an old fool after all.

And Dan slept that night with the southernwood under his pillow and dreamt of dominoes and blackbirds, clary sage and rosemary and rue.

Chapter 5

THE APRIL days grew imperceptibly longer. Sometimes they were grey with high winds and showers of driving rain, but when the sun shone it was hot enough to make the earth steam. In the damp warmth everything grew. Pat's raspberry canes were in full leaf, and so were the hawthorn and elder bushes in the hedges. Jim and George were busy spreading fertilizer and sowing, and the winter wheat was nearly high enough to take the roller over it: Dan's beans were just showing above ground, the pear trees were in blossom, and in the woods where Dan walked with Ben, the dog's mercury had disappeared among the wind-flowers and the green spears of the blue-bells.

Living in a town, and spending the days in school, Dan had never really noticed the spring before; but here on the farm where the work was tied to the seasons, it could not be ignored.

To give the men more time, he and Pat took over most of the yard work, feeding the pigs and the calves, and starting the evening milking together when Jim and George were late. Dan fetched the cows in by himself now, for there was rarely any traffic down the lane, and though he was still not strong enough to lift the churns, he could switch on the engine in the dairy, and make sure everything was ready.

'It's not always as busy as this,' explained Pat one morning as they mixed buckets of pig swill outside the

kitchen door. 'But there's always a rush at this time of year, when everything seems to need doing at once. Then there's a slack time, and after that there's a rush again with the haymaking and harvest. Honestly Dan, it's marvellous having you here to help. You've learnt so quickly and the work is much easier when there are two of you.'

Dan glowed. 'It doesn't seem like work to me. I like it.' He gave the swill another vigorous stir, and inspected it critically. 'There, that looks all right. What shall I do now?' He grinned at her. 'I've got to earn my keep.'

Pat pushed the hair out of her eyes and stood upright, rubbing the small of her back.

'You'll be earning a wage at this rate,' she laughed. 'Oh, thank goodness that's done. I hate bending over those buckets. Let's get the pigs fed, and then perhaps you could go and get the eggs while I do the vegetables for dinner. Here, you take the smallest bucket or you'll hurt that tum of yours.'

There were eight pigs, four in each sty, half grown and boisterous. At the sound of the clinking buckets they tumbled, squealing, towards the troughs, shoving and pushing for the best places. Dan thought the swill looked and smelt disgusting, but they guzzled it, burying their flat pink noses and making horrible slurping noises.

'It's enough to put you off bacon for ever!' he said, scraping his bucket into the trough. 'I'll get the basket and fetch the eggs. I think I prefer hens to pigs.'

Pat watched him through the kitchen window as he went over to the hen houses, gaily swinging his basket. He seemed a different boy now to the white nervous child who had arrived on that cold spring evening. He was so much fitter, and had put on weight, thank goodness, but, she decided, the change went deeper than that. She remembered waking in the night to the small sound of his crying and forcing herself to lie still because she knew how hard he was trying to hide his unhappiness. Well, he was sleeping soundly now; and she smiled as she thought of the precious, tattered piece of southernwood. Ben Huggett was an extraordinary old man. She wondered if he was just a good psychologist or whether he really believed that the herb could heal. Not that it mattered. For Dan, it had all the properties of a magic charm, and so of course it worked.

She wished his other troubles could be solved as simply, but she was afraid it would be a long time before his family stopped thinking of him as a failure. She was fond of her brother Geoff, but she still felt angry when she remembered the way he had talked about Dan. What did a family firm matter compared with Dan's happiness! She wished they could see the confident way he worked on the farm and realize how sensible and reliable he was. Surely that was as important as passing exams.

'He's really at home here,' she thought, 'I'm going to miss him dreadfully.'

The outline of the potato she was peeling wavered and she dropped it into the bowl and searched angrily for her handkerchief. Oh damn, she must not get upset. She had fought a hard battle with herself before she had finally accepted the fact that she could not have children; fought it and won. Now she could even nurse Mrs George's babies without a qualm. But Dan was different.

'All right, Pat Knott,' she said. 'Let's face up to it. You love him and you wish he was yours. But he isn't and there's nothing you can do about it. So pull yourself together, and get these blasted potatoes peeled!'

She blew her nose, and reached determinedly for the knife. Jim would not thank her if dinner was late, and it would never do if Dan came back and found her crying.

She need not have worried for Dan was taking his time. The ability to dawdle was one of the things he was learning from Ben Huggett.

'Go easy now,' the old man kept telling him. 'You rush round like a whirligig and you won't see for the dust. Stand quiet and look and listen, that's the way to learn.'

It was easy advice to follow, particularly on a sunny morning. The hen houses were the old-fashioned kind, for Pat only kept a couple of dozen fowls. They smelt strongly of creosote and hen, and had flaps at the back which opened on to the nesting boxes. Dan handled the eggs carefully, liking the feel of the smooth shells in the palm of his hand. Some of them were already cold but one or two were still warm, and on one of the nests a hen was still sitting, feathers fluffed out and eyes blinking rapidly as it concentrated on the serious business of laying.

'Lazy old thing,' said Dan. 'You're late!' and gently shut the flap. He might as well wait until she had finished.

Some of the hens laid wild, preferring the hedge bottoms

and long grass to the safety of the nesting boxes. Dan knew the favourite places and went to check them. He found three more eggs but at the fourth place someone or something had arrived before him. The egg had been eaten, and only the broken shell was left.

'I wonder who did that?' he thought. 'I must remember to ask Mr 'Uggett. He's sure to know.'

There was still no sound from the hen house so he left the egg basket in the shade and wandered across the field which was very small, and was only used for the hens. The cows were turned into it occasionally to keep the grass down, but Auntie Pat had told him that she wouldn't let Uncle Jim plough it up because it grew mushrooms in the late summer and cowslips in the spring. Everywhere he walked now he could see the ribbed leaves and thick stems with their clusters of closed buds, and was glad Auntie Pat had kept them safe. It wasn't just that they looked pretty; he had tried her cowslip wine and even Uncle Jim agreed that it was worth the loss of the field.

A rough path led across the field from the yard, deeply rutted where the tractor wheels had sunk into the ground during the winter, and now caked hard by the sun. The deepest ruts still had water in them and Dan was horrified to find one which a frog had mistakenly decided was a safe place to lay its spawn. The water was rapidly drying up, the top layer of spawn was a disintegrating mess, but worst of all some of it had hatched, and in the muddy residue was a cluster of exhausted tadpoles. Fascinated, Dan watched them struggling to push their way into the deepest part of the water. There was already a ring of small black corpses on the mud round the edge, and it was obvious that the others wouldn't last long. By the end of the day all the water would have gone.

He was wondering how and where to move them when a triumphant cackle from the hen house told him that at

last the lazy hen had laid. He collected her egg, and deciding that he needed help with his rescue operation went as quickly as the full basket allowed back to the house.

Pat listened sympathetically to his description of the tadpoles.

'Just let me look at my stew, and I'll come and give you a hand,' she said. She looked in the cupboard under the sink and found a plastic bucket.

'Leave the eggs on the table for now, and take this out to the water trough and half fill it. Tadpoles don't like tap water, but the trough water should be all right. I won't be long, I promise.'

By the time he had fetched the water she was ready and they set off across the field. The water in the rut seemed to be shallower than when Dan had left it, and the tadpoles were definitely more exhausted, only the occasional convulsive wriggle showing they were still alive.

'It's fantastic,' said Pat, kneeling down to stare at them. 'Like watching the beginning of the world. It must have been just like this when life began; the sun drying up the water and all the creatures in the sea fighting to survive.'

'And then one of them grew legs and crept out on to the mud, just like tadpoles do.'

'That's right; but an awful lot must have died like these will if we don't do something about them quickly. Here, I brought a couple of wooden spoons. Fish the frog-spawn out into the bucket and then we'll catch the tadpoles.'

They scooped them up in twos and threes and dropped them into the deep water, and almost immediately they revived, wriggling their tails and swimming down to the bottom of the bucket and back to the top, to hang motionless but very much alive just below the surface of the water.

'Now what?' said Dan, when they had picked up all the ones which showed any sign of life, and a few doubtfuls for good measure.

'Well, it's no good taking them back to the house because they always seem to go mouldy and die off if you keep them indoors. Go down the track and across the next field and there's a dew pond in the far corner. There are always lots of tadpoles there so they should be all right, and you can go back in a week or two and try and find the baby frogs.'

'All right,' said Dan rather reluctantly. He would have liked to have kept them, but it seemed silly to rescue them from one death just to kill them off in another way. He knew the way to the pond, and set off, taking care not to splash the water out of the bucket. The pond was, as Auntie Pat had said, alive with tadpoles and great clots of spawn shone round the reeds at the edge. He emptied his bucket into the water, and watching the tadpoles disappear with amazing speed into the shadows of the pond weed, wondered how many would actually survive to hop through the long grass of the field and lay their spawn in the pond next year.

Dinner was a rush, because the weather forecast was bad and Uncle Jim wanted to finish the last field before the rain came. By early afternoon a thin grey cloud had covered the sky and the wind was rising. Dan knew that Ben 'Uggett was busy visiting his younger sister in Banford so it was no good going to the cottage, and it did not look very inviting outdoors anyway. He hung round the kitchen where Pat was trying to do her weekly bake, eating raisins from the packets on the table and dipping an experimental finger in all the cake mixtures until she put down her spoon in exasperation.

'Daniel Hunt,' she said. 'Get out from under my feet or I won't have a cake fit to eat. Haven't you got anything you want to do?'

'No,' said Dan.

'Right,' she said firmly. 'Then get the writing pad and a pen from the dresser drawer, go into the living-room and write a letter home. At least you can't tell me this time that you're too busy!'

'Oh Auntie Pat!' he said, dismayed, but she only pointed silently at the door, and recognizing defeat, he collected the paper and pen and left her in peace.

'Dear Mummy and Dad,' he began. 'It's a long time since I've written but we have been very busy. Uncle Jim has been sowing and Auntie Pat and me have been looking after the animals and doing the milking. I like it here very much. Auntie Pat sends me off exploring and I met a friend of Uncle Jim's called Mr 'Uggett.'

He stopped, wondering what to say next. It was impossible to explain Mr 'Uggett. He thought of all the work they did in the garden, and of the blackbird who had found another mate and was busy feeding four babies in a new nest in the apple tree. He didn't think they would be interested in that, or in the long walks they went together. How could he write about seeing a pheasant, or the way the bluebells made the woods look like a lake, or the surprise he had felt when Mr 'Uggett had picked a bunch of primroses for the blue bowl on his kitchen table? Or about Dog, or the fox they had watched slipping along the hedge in the early evening two days ago? No, he decided, it was safer to say nothing at all.

'The pond is full of tadpoles,' he wrote. 'And soon Auntie Pat wants me to help her make cowslip wine. I have tasted last year's. It is very nice and very strong.' He stuck again, and rather guiltily thought up a white lie. 'It's nearly time to fetch the cows, so I'd better stop. Lots of love to you all, from Dan.'

Well, an hour was almost nearly. He pushed the folded letter into an envelope and went back to the kitchen.

'I've finished, Auntie Pat,' he said. 'Can I scrape that bowl?' And his eyes looking at her over the top of the envelope as he licked the flap were full of mischief.

Chapter 6

THAT NIGHT the rain came, followed by a succession of cold grey days. There was mud everywhere, and Uncle Jim thanked the Lord that he had finished the field work in time, and pottered round the yard with George repairing the outbuildings and checking over machinery. The yard ran with water and Dan had to get the cows in early to give himself time to wash their muddy flanks.

Everybody seemed damp and a little disgruntled, and as Auntie Pat was spring-cleaning and obviously hating it, Dan escaped with relief to the warm cosiness of Mr 'Uggett's cottage.

'We need a bit of a wet,' the old man said consolingly when Dan arrived dripping at his back door. 'It'll change after the full moon, just you see. Now come on in and I'll make a pot of tea.'

Ben 'Uggett was right as usual. The rain disappeared with the waning moon and by the second week in May, spring had come back again. On the first fine afternoon they went out together.

'I want to stretch me legs,' said Ben. 'The damp's bad for me rheumatics and I need a bit of sun to dry me out.'

They turned right at the garden gate and walked down the lane. It was a brilliant day; the sky was a high clear blue, the leaves and grass shone, and the lane was alive with birds. Dog, glad to be out of the house at last, pranced round them with unusual skittishness and when they left the lane to climb a stile into some woodland Ben had to call him sharply to heel.

'Pheasants is nesting,' he explained to Dan, and laughed at his puzzled face. 'They don't nest in trees, Dan, none of the game birds do. They just scrape a little hole in the ground under a bramble or in the brushwood, and put a bit of dead grass in it. If I let Dog run, like as not he'll step on 'em and scare 'em silly, or go eating the eggs. And keeper would have me then for sure.'

'Keeper?' said Dan.

'That's right. All these woods, and the pheasants in 'em, belong to the Big House. The keeper watches the birds all year to see no harm comes to 'em – and in October the gentlemen come down from London and shoot 'em all.'

'That seems a bit silly,' said Dan. 'What do they do that for?'

'Sport,' said Ben caustically. 'Leastways, that's what they call it. Not much sport in it to my way of thinking, sitting there with a gun with someone driving the birds so close only a fool could miss. No skill to it all.'

'But Uncle Jim said it was ill – illegal, that's it, to shoot any wild birds. I told him about your blackbird and he got quite angry. He said you should tell the police.'

'Ar,' said Ben darkly. 'I don't hold with the police. You don't want to get mixed up with them, they ask too many questions. And it is against the law to shoot pheasants unless you own 'em, so it comes to the same thing.' He sighed. 'Pheasants make lovely eating,' he added wistfully.

Dan looked at him curiously. If all the pheasants belonged to the Big House, how did Mr 'Uggett know they made lovely eating? He opened his mouth to ask and then shut it abruptly. He had an odd feeling his question might not be welcome.

'Where are we going?' he asked instead.

'I dunno,' said Ben. 'I don't go anywhere particular. I just like to have a little look round and see how things is going along.'

'What sort of things?'

'Oh,' said Ben, looking sideways at him, poker-faced. 'Whether the grass is still growing.'

'You're teasing me!' Dan was indignant.

'You asks too many questions.'

Dan's face fell. 'Sorry,' he muttered, looking away.

Ben frowned at him, puzzled. The boy was like a badly handled dog; one sharp word and he'd slink off with his tail between his legs. Wasn't natural, not in a young lad, wasn't right, and he didn't like to see it.

'Get along with you,' he said kindly. 'I was full of questions at your age. And when you're young you want to know where you're going. Time enough to watch the grass grow when you're an old man like me. So let's think now; where shall we go?'

'Is it very far to the Big House?' Dan asked tentatively. 'I've never seen a Big House.'

'It's too far by the lane. You wouldn't get back for the milking. Still . . .' Ben considered the problem. 'Can you walk real quiet?' he asked, making up his mind.

'I can try!'

'Now listen careful.' Ben leant closer and lowered his voice. 'If we cut through here to where the wood drops down to the valley, we can see right across to the Big House; see it better than you can from the lane. But soon as we step off this path we're on private land, and if they catch us they'll run us in for trespass.'

'Trespass!' Dan's eyes were wide with excitement.

'Ar; so we don't get caught, see!'

'But, Mr 'Uggett,' Dan looked at the ground under the trees, thick with dead leaves and littered with sticks and broken branches. 'They'll hear us walking. They're bound to.'

Ben shook his head. 'They won't,' he said. 'Follow me careful. Move nice and slow and put your feet down flat,

49

so your weight shifts even like.' He chuckled softly. 'And no questions,' he said.

'No questions!' said Dan happily. 'And I'll do my best, though I don't know whether I'll be very good at it.'

'You'll do,' Ben said confidently. 'Just follow me close; and if anyone comes, stand still.'

He hissed between his teeth to the waiting Dog, beckoned Dan with a jerk of his head and slipped silently into the wood, Dog and boy close at his heels. He moved as though he was weightless, the only sound the faint whisper of leaves beneath his feet, and Dan blundering behind felt like an elephant.

'Feet flat,' he told himself, trying to keep one eye on Ben 'Uggett and one on the ground ahead so that he wouldn't step on a dry twig. 'And shift your weight even like.' There must be a knack to it, he decided, but if Mr 'Uggett thought he could do it he could. He walked on, concentrating desperately, and suddenly found that it worked. He still could not move silently, but he no longer sounded like an army, and if he looked up a little instead of at his feet, he could see and avoid low branches as well as the debris on the ground. Ben looked back once to give him an approving nod and his confidence soared.

Their progress was erratic, an apparently aimless wandering from tree to tree; but Dan soon realized that they were in fact following a very faint track which avoided the roughest ground and the worst of the undergrowth, but kept roughly in the same direction. They skirted several small clearings and slid down a steep muddy bank, which Ben, knees bent, managed easily; but Dan after the first skid negotiated it on his bottom, ignoring Ben's silent laughter. Once a loud rustle and a snapping twig made them stop abruptly, but it was only a blackbird scuffing at the leaves, and they moved on, slowly so they would not frighten it. A blackbird's alarum call, Dan knew, could be heard a long way away.

At last the trees thinned and Dan realized they were coming to the end of the wood. Ben stopped and waited for him to come close, and his voice when he spoke was hardly more than a whisper.

'Nearly there now,' he said. 'But go careful. The trees thin out and that red jersey of yours'll show up like a lamp. There's not much cover at the edge there, and keeper lives just below.'

Dan looked down at his jersey. It was not new, but even after several washings it was still a very bright red, the worst possible colour if you did not want to be seen. He rubbed his hand thoughtfully across the seat of his filthy jeans and decided a bit more dirt now would not make much difference.

'Can't we crawl?' he asked.

Ben Huggett sighed deeply and shook his head.

'I must be out of my mind,' he said. 'All right, we crawl. Dog, stay here.'

With surprising agility he dropped on all fours, and then, flat on his stomach, inched himself forward.

'Golly,' thought Dan, copying him. 'He's much better than me, and much quicker.' He arrived, breathless, beside him. 'Where did you learn . . . ?' he began, and stopped. No questions, he remembered, catching Ben's eye, and no questions it would be.

'Well, there you are,' whispered Ben. 'I hopes it was worth it.'

They were lying on a patch of tussocky grass at the top of a steep slope. On either side the wood curved round and down into the valley, but the ground in front of them fell away sharply and then levelled off into fields where cattle were grazing. The air was very clear after the rain, and they could see the road at the bottom of the valley, the river glinting in the sun, and the green tracery of the trees on the other side. And just below them, where the fields ended, was the Big House.

Yes, it was worth it, Dan thought. It was the most beautiful house he had ever seen. He had expected a tall, grim building like a castle, not this friendly sprawling place, rose coloured and higgledy-piggledy, with small paned windows, red tiled roof and twisted chimney pots.

'Gosh, it is big,' he said. 'All those roofs, like a pushed together village.'

'Well I reckon it is almost a village,' said Ben. 'That's all stables on the left there, and beyond the yard, that's the home farm; and all that lot there,' he pointed, 'that's where the gardeners and the farm folk live. And Mr Jones the keeper. He can look straight up here from his sitting-room window.'

Instinctively Dan pressed himself closer down into the grass.

'Who lives in the Big House?' he asked.

'No one since the old man died,' said Ben sadly. 'His own lad was killed in the war; he had to leave it all to relations in London. They only comes for the shooting, or weekends sometimes. 'Tisn't the same.'

'You mean they could live here all the time and they'd rather live in London?' Dan could not believe anyone could be such a fool.

'Well, they're city folk,' said Ben as if that explained everything. 'Come along now, time to move. This grass is as wet as a ditch.'

The walk back seemed colder and longer, probably, Dan decided, because of the uncomfortable damp patches down the front of his jersey and jeans, and because Ben 'Uggett was walking very fast indeed. It was difficult to keep up with him and still move quietly; and now the excitement of seeing the house was over he was more aware of the fact that he was deliberately trespassing. He felt horribly nervous and sure that at any minute they would hear the yell and crashing footsteps of the keeper.

In fact he was very glad indeed when they came out of the wood into a sunny field beside a path which he recognized as the proper footpath which led back to the land and Ben 'Uggett's cottage.

The old man was waiting a little way ahead and smiled as he came panting up.

'Went too fast for you, did I?' he asked, still keeping his voice low.

'I make so much noise when I hurry. I'll never learn to be as quiet as you and Dog.'

'Course you will.' Ben seemed surprised. 'You managed grand for the first time off. Were you frightened?'

'Yes,' Dan admitted, honestly but reluctantly. 'A bit on the way back.'

'Good,' said Ben. 'It's best to be frightened. It keeps you careful.'

'Were you frightened too?' asked Dan, astonished.

'Well, I still watch what I'm doing,' he said. 'That way you don't make mistakes.'

'But do you often trespass, Mr 'Uggett?' The question was out before he could stop it and he reddened and said 'Sorry, perhaps I shouldn't ask you that.'

Ben Huggett smiled. 'Let's just say I go where I feel like going.'

Dan grinned back. 'That does sound better,' he agreed. 'Anyway I'm glad because otherwise I wouldn't have seen the Big House.'

'Did you like it then?'

'Yes. It was lovely.' He thought for a bit. 'But the garden wasn't as nice as yours, even though it's so much bigger.'

'Ah, you should have seen it in the old days,' Ben said. 'It's all labour saving now, shrubs and things but it was a picture then, any time of year. Things have changed since old Squire's day and there's some he counted his friends who aren't welcome there now.'

He strode down the path frowning blackly, and Dan followed bursting with curiosity, but for once having the sense to keep quiet.

'Ah well,' said Ben at last, 'new days, new ways. Still,' he grinned wickedly at Dan, 'Keeper Jones can put up his fences. He don't keep me out.'

Dan stared at him completely bewildered, and at the sight of his puzzled face Ben laughed outright.

'You're a good lad, Dan; don't you mind my moods,' he said. 'I've tales I can tell you when there's time but not today. Don't be late for milking today. We don't want people asking where you've been.'

They stopped at the cottage gate to say goodbye.

'And thank you Mr 'Uggett,' said Dan, 'for a super afternoon. And I'm going to practise walking like that at home, then perhaps I'll be quieter next time. That is,' he looked hopefully at Ben, 'if there is a next time.'

'Well,' said Ben thoughtfully, 'you never know when things will come in useful. But don't let anyone see you at it, mind.'

'Oh, of course not.' They looked at each other with unspoken understanding. 'Goodbye Mr 'Uggett and thank you again. I'll see you soon.'

But he had only gone a few yards down the lane when Ben's voice stopped him once more.

'Oh, Dan,' he said. 'Next time, you wear a nice dark jersey, see. That red is terrible bright.'

Chapter 7

THE KITCHEN windows were covered with steam from the washing machine. Newly washed sheets flapped briskly on the line under the apple trees, and the back door was closed against the sharp west wind. Jim reached the porch thankfully and pushed the door hard with his shoulder, trying to open it. His hands were covered with black grease from the mower blades, and blood dripped steadily from a deep cut on his right forefinger in spite of the grimy handkerchief he had wrapped hastily round it. The door stayed shut.

'Pat,' he yelled, 'For goodness' sake open this door,' and thumped it again with his shoulder to try and make her hear.

She opened it so quickly he nearly fell in. The usually ordered kitchen was a shambles and she was obviously feeling as bad tempered as he was.

'Can't you open it yourself?' she snapped crossly.

'No,' he said, and held out his hand. The blood had soaked through the handkerchief and was running stickily down his forearm.

'Oh my God,' she said. 'What on earth have you done? Here, sit down.' She hooked a chair out from the table with her foot and pushed him into it.

'Hold it up and try not to drip on the table. Honestly, what a time to go and cut yourself.'

'Thanks for the sympathy! I didn't have much choice.' He glared at her.

'Don't be childish,' she said. 'How can I be sympathetic when I'm in the middle of this lot?' She waved a wet hand vaguely at the pile of dirty washing, the washing machine and the sink full of rinsing water. 'And I've still got a meal to cook,' she added grabbing a towel from the dresser. 'Where the hell's the first aid box?' She flung open a cupboard door and started rummaging noisily through the assortment of things on the shelf.

'Here, steady on,' Jim protested as a pile of baking tins hit the floor. 'It's not in there, it's in the left-hand drawer.'

'Then why didn't you say so? Anyway I'm looking for the Swarfega. I'll have to clean the grease off you before I do the cut. How bad is it?'

'Pretty bad,' he said casually.

She turned sharply. 'Hospital?' she asked.

'I don't think so. Not if you can stop it bleeding. You'd better have a look.'

She dumped the first aid kit on the table and carefully removed the sodden handkerchief. It was a nasty jagged gash, deep and still oozing blood.

'That needs stitching,' she said flatly.

'Oh, for goodness' sake, Pat!'

'Well, it does. It's filthy dirty and too deep to leave like that. I'll clean it up and take you into hospital. How on earth did you do it?'

'Trying to move a bolt on the mower. The wrench slipped.'

'Then you'll need a tetanus injection as well, so it's no good arguing. Honestly, this is the last straw.'

She set to work in angry silence and Jim, feeling very ill-used, was delighted when the door opened and George appeared.

'What's the damage then, Mr Knott?' he asked anxiously.

'Pat's all for rushing me to hospital. I think she's making a fuss,' he said, and was annoyed when George nodded wisely and said,

'Quite right too, Mrs Knott. I thought it was a bad 'un when he did it. You take him off to hospital and get it seen to.'

'But it'll stop me working for at least a week if I have it stitched,' Jim protested.

'Do that anyway,' said George calmly. 'You'd have to keep it wrapped up and clean, stitches or no. Now don't fret yourself, I can manage fine; and Dan can help me with most things.' He smiled at Pat. 'He's coming on a treat, Mrs Knott. Turn his hand to anything and glad to do it.' He chuckled quietly. 'And if the worst comes to the worst, you can always come out too and leave Mr Knott here to do the housework. Nice clean job that is!'

'All right, George,' agreed Jim reluctantly.

'Well, I'd better get you to hospital then,' said Pat, and looked despairingly round the untidy kitchen. George looked at it too.

'Why don't you make a cup of tea, Mrs Knott?' he suggested. 'And leave all this. I'll pop down and have a word with my missus and get her to come and tidy up for you while you're gone. And if Dan gets back before you do I'll let him know where you are. Now get that kettle on.' And he shut the door firmly behind him before she could argue.

She watched him trudge steadily across the yard and turned with a rather watery smile to Jim, who was awkwardly ladling tea into the pot with his left hand.

'I'm sorry, love.' She took the teapot from him and pushed him gently back on to his chair.

'Have you had an awful morning?' he asked sympathetically.

'Yes.' She handed him his mug of tea and sat down

59

thankfully with her own. 'I meant to get all this finished early but first Mrs George came in for her eggs and Dan hadn't brought them so I had to go and find him; and then he wanted to go down to Ben Huggett and refused to wear his red jersey so I spent hours trying to find him another. He was furious because I had washed his old green one. I had to lend him one of mine.' She was still indignant at the time spent burrowing through her drawers while Dan rejected each jersey she suggested. 'The only one he'd wear was the brown one I'd put for the jumble sale, and it took me ages to find it. And I burnt my cake and I didn't get the washing done and you came in dripping blood so I lost my temper.' She finished with a rush.

'And now you're going to take me to hospital,' said Jim, pulling her to her feet. 'And when you come back Mrs George will have everything tidy.' He hugged her quickly. 'All right?'

'Yes,' she said, and hugged him back.

'But I still wish I knew what had got into Dan,' she said as they drove out through the yard gate. 'There's nothing wrong with his red jersey; and do you know what he was doing when I found him this morning? Just walking round and round in circles on the dry straw in the stock yard.'

'Was he now,' said Jim thoughtfully, and Pat with her eyes on the road missed the grin of sudden understanding which crossed his face.

'Did you ask him what he was doing?'

'Well, no,' she admitted reluctantly, 'I don't like to chivvy him, he gets too much of that at home.' She changed gear with sudden ferocity. 'Oh Jim, why can't they leave him alone? Can't they see the damage they have done trying to make him like the other two? Why can't they let him go his own way and just be himself? It's not his fault he didn't pass that exam. He wasn't well, and he gets nervous and they pushed him too hard. Can't we talk to them and try to make them understand before he has to go back?'

'No,' said Jim firmly. 'That's Dan's battle, not ours.' He could feel her disappointment and paused, trying to find the best way to explain it to her. 'You told me that when you and Geoff were young he always did everything better than you, and that he couldn't bear it if he didn't succeed at everything he tried. He sets the same standard for his children, and he's been lucky; the twins are like him and they reach that standard. But Dan's like you, the odd one out, struggling along in the wake of the twins, and losing what little confidence he has because he can't keep up with them. It's none of our business to try and alter his family; but we can send him back to them knowing that for the first time he can do things that they can't do, that he understands things they don't understand. We can give him confidence, and then he can fight his own battles. Once he can do that he won't mind being different.'

Pat thought about it. 'It sounds all right,' she said. 'But are we really doing it?'

'Yes.' Jim had no doubts. 'And what we don't provide, Ben Huggett will.' He thought of Dan walking carefully round in circles on the crackling straw of the barn and smiled to himself. He had served his apprenticeship with Ben when he was about Dan's age, and he knew what Dan had been doing. Perhaps it was just as well, he thought with amusement, that Pat didn't know. And possibly Dan himself hadn't yet discovered the trade Ben followed; but he would when the old man thought he was ready.

'I think we're in for an interesting summer,' he said reflectively.

Dan, blissfully unaware of the speculation he was arousing, was enjoying himself. He had been a bit worried when Auntie Pat caught him practising his walk, but he had got away with it, and he was very proud of getting his own way over the jersey. It was a bit big, but not noticeably so if he rolled up the sleeves, and like his jeans, was well washed to a suitably nondescript colour. Anyway Mr 'Uggett had nodded approvingly when he saw it, so he felt it had been worth making Auntie Pat a bit cross. After all he could not expect her to understand that his jersey was more important than getting on with the housework, though he was sorry she had burnt her cake.

When he arrived, Mr 'Uggett was busy in the garden. Dan was continually amazed by the amount of work it demanded. The one at home was quite small, just lawn and rosebushes and plants bought from the shop to go along the edges of the rose beds. He had not realized that a proper garden needed all this digging and manuring and weeding.

He went as usual on a quick tour of inspection before he started work. His beans were coming on nicely, and so were the lettuce in their glass tunnels. The daffodils were over. He had watched, fascinated, while the buds, which had been pointing skywards had swelled a little more each day until they had gradually bent over and become tipped with bright yellow as the flower pushed through. Now they had withered, but the honeysuckle was in full leaf, hiding the 'doings' completely, and the fruit trees were smothered in blossom.

Another crop of weeds had appeared in the vegetable patch, so without having to be told, he fetched the hoe and worked his way carefully down the rows of young carrots and peas, the perennial spinach and his own much prized beans. Hoeing still made his arms ache but each time he tried to go on longer before taking a rest, because Mr 'Uggett always seemed tireless and had told him it was only practice. He fancied his arm muscles were stronger since he had started gardening. It would be nice if they grew like George's and Uncle Jim's; a knotted bulge under the skin. He stopped and flexed one, but he couldn't really see it under the loose jersey.

'That'll do now,' said Ben as he got to the end of the row. 'That's how I like to see a bit of garden. Good clean earth and no weeds messing it about. Those beans of yours'll do well if we keep 'em clear of blackfly. Now go and get that hoe cleaned up and we'll be off out for a bit.'

They went through the wood at the back of the cottage, towards the field where they had first met. This, Dan knew, was safe ground, but even so they moved quietly and kept their voices low, and without being told Dog stayed at heel. It was a nicer wood than the one above Big House, with patches of wild flowers and late primroses, and in the open spaces between the trees they could hardly walk without treading on bluebells.

'Mr 'Uggett,' asked Dan. 'Will we be coming back this way? Because I think I might pick some bluebells for Auntie Pat.' Ben cocked an enquiring eyebrow and he went rather pink. 'Well, there was a bit of trouble over jerseys,' he explained. 'And perhaps it might be a good idea to take her something.'

'Perhaps it might,' Ben agreed solemnly, and they grinned at each other.

At the edge of the wood the wind hit them. They had been sheltered in the garden and among the trees, but here it swept across the open fields bringing tears to Dan's eyes.

'My, that's stronger than I thought,' said Ben, clutching his battered hat. 'We'd best go down by the river, it won't be so bad down there.'

Heads bent they headed across the fields and down into the valley, where the steep rise of the further bank protected them. The clouds raced across the blue sky, and above their heads a kestrel hovered shining copper-coloured in the sunlight.

'I love the wind,' said Dan.

So did Dog. He was still obediently at heel, but impatience showed in every line of his body, for the wind brought him, tantalizing and overpowering, the smell of rabbit.

'Off you go then,' said Ben, and he was away, streaking across the rough grass, nose to the ground. Dan ran after him but soon returned panting.

'He's too fast for me,' he gasped.

'Ar, you won't catch that one,' Ben agreed. 'It's the greyhound in him. He's a good dog, obedient; he needs a stretch like this now and then.'

He circled back to them, tongue lolling, and then was away once more. The rabbits had gone to ground, but a covey of six partridges broke cover and he chased them vainly until they disappeared over a hedge and then turning abruptly, raced for the river.

'Dog!' yelled Ben, but he was too late. With a splash and a flurry Dog was in the water swimming strongly in pursuit of a floating branch.

'Come out of it,' said Ben sternly, and Dog came, showering them with water as he shook himself dry.

'Damn and blast!' said Ben, jumping out of the way but Dan, helpless with laughter, could not move. Pleased with himself, Dog was off again, round and round, through the rough grass, tail tucked in and hindquarters bunched under him in a most extraordinary way.

'What's the matter with him?' gasped Dan, still laughing.

'Got the wind up his bum,' said Ben dourly, brushing himself down. 'Knows he shouldn't have gone in the river. He'll sober down in a bit.'

He did; and was soon trotting beside them again, confin-

ing himself to an occasional pounce into the thick tussocks of dry dead grass which edged the path, sniffing deeply and scrabbling at them with his forepaws.

'What's he looking for?' asked Dan.

'Mice,' said Ben, and parting the grass showed him the round hole leading into the earth.

'Does he ever catch any?'

'No, they're too quick for 'im, but he never learns,' Ben chuckled. 'Look at him now, the old fool!'

Dog was stalking a tussock with immense care, crouched low and placing each foot with cat-like precision. Close to it he froze, ears pricked, and then leapt straight into the middle of it, forcing a way in among the tangled stems. There was a sudden flurry, a sharp cry, and with a heave he emerged triumphant with something white in his mouth that wriggled and screamed high and shrill.

Dan stayed where he was, so surprised he could not move, but Ben reached Dog in two swift strides.

'Keep,' he commanded sharply and Dog stood quivering, his head shaken by the animal's effort to escape. From one of his pockets Ben produced a battered pair of gloves, slipped them on, and reached for the animal in Dog's mouth.

'Give,' he said. A moment later he had straightened up with the animal in his hands. 'Good lad, stay.' And slowly Dog lay down, still quivering with excitement, his eyes fixed intently on Ben.

'Well dang me!' The old man drew a deep breath and whistled softly with astonishment. 'Come and see here.'

Dan ran to join him. 'What is it, Mr 'Uggett? What is it?' He was as excited as Dog.

Silently Ben held out his hands so Dan could see, but Dan was no wiser. It was a strange creature, short-legged and long-bodied, quite small and covered with thick yellow-white fur; and it glared back at Dan with fierce

66

scarlet eyes. As he watched it began to struggle again, darting its head as it tried to bite Ben's restraining hands, but,

'Its mouth's tied up,' cried Dan horrified, and looking up saw Ben's face was a mask of anger.

'Yes,' he said shortly, and swore under his breath. For a few minutes he stood still thinking hard with Dan shocked into silence beside him, and then he made up his mind.

'This needs seeing to,' he said. 'We'd best get off home.'

One handed he unbuttoned his jacket and fumbled with the lining. A quick movement and the little animal had disappeared inside and the jacket was re-buttoned. Meeting Dan's astonished gaze Ben cleared his throat and then winked at him.

'It's a pocket,' he said. 'It'll lie quiet in there in the dark. Come on now.' And he set off across the field.

Dan ran after him. 'Please Mr 'Uggett,' he begged. 'Please tell me what it is. I've never seen one before.'

The old man stopped and looked at him. 'Haven't you?' he asked surprised, and then shook his head slowly. 'No, I don't suppose you would 'ave. It's a ferret, Dan, that's what it is. A ferret.'

Chapter 8

DAN WAS out of breath when they arrived at the cottage. Ben never seemed to hurry, but he covered the ground at a steady pace which never varied, uphill or down, and had Dan half running to keep up. Straight up the garden path they went and in at the back door; and then to Dan's amazement Ben calmly hung up his hat and sat down in the rocking chair by the stove.

'But aren't you going to untie its mouth? Aren't you going to see if it's all right?' he asked urgently. 'We can't leave it like that.'

'Hold up,' said Ben. 'First things first. Sit down a minute and we'll talk things over. We've got problems here.'

Dan pulled out a chair and perched on the edge of it. 'What problems?' he asked crossly. It seemed quite simple to him. Here was a small animal that someone had ill-treated. Obviously it was up to them to put things right, so what was Mr 'Uggett waiting for.

'It's easy enough to untie its mouth, Dan. But what do we do with it after that?'

'Oh!' said Dan blankly. He saw now what Mr 'Uggett was getting at.

'Feed it?' he suggested tentatively.

'All right, so we feed it. And then what?'

There was a long pause. Dan, no longer cross, settled back in his chair, thinking hard. Yes, they *had* got a problem; and he did not really know anything about ferrets which made it even more difficult.

'I see,' he said slowly. 'Do we keep it, or do we let it go? Is that what you mean?'

'That's it, Dan, that's what we've got to decide. Do we set it free in the wood and let it take its chance, or do we feed it and look after it?'

'But it's not a wild animal, is it? Wouldn't it die on its own in the wood?'

'Maybe. Maybe not. Ferrets is funny creatures. They're never far from wild unless you handle them right and they learn to know you. This one's been handled bad; it'd probably manage.'

'You don't sound very sure.'

'You can't be sure. If it's strong enough and clever enough it'll kill and eat. If not, it'll get killed; that's the way it goes. It's the same on the farm, Dan. Your Uncle Jim only keeps the best of the stock, the others go to the butcher. You can't be soft-hearted in the country or you upset everything.'

There was a long pause while Dan thought that over. It was, he realized, quite true and perfectly sensible, and yet . . .

'Does it cost much to keep a ferret?' he asked, not quite looking at Ben and trying very hard to keep his voice casual.

'Not very much,' Ben was equally casual. 'Bread and milk and a bit of meat now and then; bit of hay to sleep in. Of course you need a hutch; a good strong one with a wire door. That can cost a bit.'

'Oh,' said Dan. 'A hutch.'

He thought his pocket money would run to bread and milk and maybe a bit of meat, but a hutch was different. Perhaps he could find some wood at the farm and make one if Mr 'Uggett had something he could use just for now? Anyway it was worth the risk. He took a deep breath to give him courage.

'Please, Mr 'Uggett,' he pleaded. 'Can't we keep him? He didn't look very strong and he wasn't clever enough to get away from Dog; and I'd pay out of my pocket money, and it just seems so awful when we saved him once to let him go and get killed and I'm sorry if it's soft-hearted but I would like to keep him very much, because I've never had anything of my own that was alive.'

He stopped to get his breath and waited tense with longing. It seemed a long time before Ben looked up.

'Well,' he said slowly. 'It wouldn't do any harm to feed him up and see how he handles. But mind now, I'm a busy man. You're the one who'll have to look after him. He's your ferret, not mine.'

'Oh I'll do everything! I promise!' His cheeks were scarlet with excitement. 'Thank you Mr 'Uggett, thank you *very* much.'

'Get along with you.' Ben seemed almost embarrassed. 'To tell truth I'm partial to ferrets,' he grinned wickedly. 'Though there's some as wouldn't be pleased to know I'm keeping one. Now,' he said briskly changing the subject, 'we'd best get things sorted. It's just crossed my mind that there may be an old hutch in that shed by the "doings". I had one once, and I can't remember throwing it out. You get some milk from the larder and warm a drop on the stove while I go and look. Saucepan's on the shelf there.'

Left by himself Dan gave a small yell of triumph and did a quick victory dance across the kitchen to the larder. He had hoped he might persuade Mr 'Uggett, but never dreamed that Mr 'Uggett himself had wanted to keep the ferret.

'Hey Dog,' he said. 'We've got a ferret, Mr 'Uggett and me!' Dog thumped his tail in response to the happy note in Dan's voice, and went to sleep again.

Ben's footsteps sounded outside and he came in with a big wooden box in his arms.

'You found it?'

'I did.' Ben dumped the box on the table and went to shut the door. 'Take a look at that then.'

Dan inspected it excitedly. It was well weathered but strong, with good hinges and clasp on the wire door, roofing felt on the top, and four short legs to keep it clear of the ground. Inside a partition divided off a sleeping area and Ben had pushed into it a handful of dry bracken.

'Hadn't got any hay,' he explained. 'So I pulled some from the edge of the wood.'

'It's a super hutch, Mr 'Uggett,' said Dan, opening and shutting the door. 'Really super.'

'It's a good strong one that. I made it meself.' He patted the roof approvingly. 'Now then, let's get organized. Got that milk ready?'

'Yes, Mr 'Uggett.'

'Then get a saucer from the larder and a slice of bread from the bin and we'll get this fellow-me-lad sorted.'

'Yes, Mr 'Uggett.'

'You see,' said Ben as Dan mixed the bread and milk, 'we got to know just what we're going to do before we get him out and cut that string. Someone's treated him bad so he'll expect us to do the same. He'll be frightened and that makes 'em savage and they've got teeth on 'em like a razor. They're killers by nature and they'll bite to the bone if you give 'em the chance.'

'Golly,' said Dan wide-eyed. 'Then how are we going to do it?'

'Like this.' Ben pulled the gloves out of his pocket, put them on the table, and then got out his penknife. It was an old silver one, with rings at each end to open it, and four blades. With care he selected the smallest, very thin and fine, and ran his thumb against the edge to see how sharp it was. He nodded, satisfied, and handed it to Dan.

'Careful,' he said. 'It's got an edge on it.'

He opened the door of the hutch wide, put the saucer of food just inside, and pulled on the gloves.

'Now then,' he said. 'My hands are bigger than yours so I'll hold him. He'll try and struggle and he's got to be kept still. Soon as his mouth is free I'll push him in the hutch and you stand by to shut the door quick.'

Dan looked down at the penknife and gulped.

'You mean I've got to cut the string?' he asked aghast. 'But I don't know how to do it. The knife's too sharp. I'll cut him.'

'Course you won't,' said Ben calmly. 'Wouldn't tell you to do it if I thought you'd hurt him.' He held out one hand with the fingers bunched into a point. 'Look,' he explained, taking the knife. 'Don't saw at it with the edge towards him. Slip it in sideways like this.'

He ran the flat of the blade against his fingers, turned it a little and flicked it outwards. 'See?' he asked.

Dumbly Dan nodded, and took the knife again, swallowing hard. He was terrified that his hand would shake, that the string would be too tough, that he would cut the ferret's mouth, that . . .

'Right,' said Ben. 'Here we go then.' And giving Dan no time for further protests or panic he reached inside his jacket and pulled out the ferret.

It struggled under his hand, back legs raking against the table top and the muscles of the long back bunching convulsively. Unhurried and steady as a rock Ben moved his grip, turning it on its side, one hand firm across body and legs, the other pinning its head and shoulders. It quivered but was still.

'Now,' he said.

The thread was very thin and the yellow fur was specked red where the ferret had worried at it to free itself. Dan laid the flat of the knife against its muzzle. The first two strands were cruelly tight and not even the tip of the blade

73

would slip under them, but the last one crossing the corner of its mouth looked as if it had a bit more play to it.

He was too absorbed now to be nervous. Under the tips of his fingers, searching for the thread he could feel the warmth of fur and the tiny movements of cheek muscles flinching away from his touch. It smelt rank. He had never realized before that you could smell fear. His fingers found the thread. He could just grip it with the edge of his nails but there was no room for the knife. He looked quickly up at Ben.

'Hold him still,' he said. 'I'll have to pull it to get the knife under. It's going to hurt him.'

Ben nodded. 'I've got him,' he said.

Quickly Dan pulled on the thread and slipped the thin blade under it. He felt the ferret's head jerk with pain, and then he had the knife edge against the thread and with one quick outward stroke cut it in two.

'Watch out!' said Ben sharply, and Dan moved his hands just in time. Free at last, the ferret struck like a snake, its little yellow fangs gleaming. It missed Dan's fingers by a hair's breadth, but as Ben shifted his grip to lift it into the hutch it twisted sideways and struck again, sinking its teeth into the leather glove with a silent ferocity that made Dan gasp.

Ben swore violently under his breath and bundled it backwards into the cage. He shook his hand hard, trying to free it but the ferret clung grimly on while Dan, overcome by the release from tension and the sight of his invincible Mr 'Uggett beaten by such a small opponent, doubled up, hooting with laughter.

'It's all right for you, it's not your fingers!' Ben was not amused. 'Now come on, we're not done yet.'

Still giggling Dan pulled himself together and got ready to shut the door. Ben pushed the ferret further back into the cage, let it go, and as quickly and smoothly as he could, drew his hands away, leaving the glove in the cage with the ferret holding on to it. Dan fastened the door and they looked at each other with satisfaction.

'We did that jolly well, I think,' said Dan. He giggled again. 'But you did look funny.'

'Maybe I did then,' said Ben with a reluctant grin, rubbing his sore fingers. There were two little red blood spots where the canines had just managed to pierce the leather, and he sucked them ruefully.

'There's nothing wrong with its teeth anyway.'

They stood and watched it with admiration. Feeling the unexpected lightness of the glove it worried at it, shaking it to and fro like a terrier with a rat, and then suddenly let it go and stood glaring at them with hot scarlet eyes, chittering angrily. Then as neither of them moved, it gradually relaxed and began tentatively to explore the hutch, standing on hind legs to sniff at the roof and into the corners, and testing the wire door with its forepaws. At last, satisfied that there was no danger, it deigned to inspect the saucer of food, finally settling to eat with a daintiness Dan found amazing.

'He'll do all right now,' said Ben confidently, and went to put the kettle on. But Dan stayed watching fascinated as the ferret worked its way through the bread and milk, stopping now and then to stare back at him, the milk dripping from its chin. At last, its stomach visibly swollen, it burrowed into the bracken, circled round to make a hollow and went to sleep.

With a deep sigh of happiness Dan went and sat down.

'Now,' he said, taking the mug of tea Ben had poured out for him. 'Tell me all about ferrets.'

'Don't want much, do you?' Ben's face crinkled with amusement. 'Where shall I begin?'

'Well, what are they? What do people use them for? Why was its mouth tied? Why . . . ?'

'Hey, that's enough to start with,' Ben protested. He put down his mug and settled himself more comfortably in his rocking chair.

'They're kind of first cousins to the stoats and weasels, and you get two kinds,' he said. 'The yellow ones like ours, and the little brown ones. Polecats some people call them. Fierce little devils, the lot of 'em, but you can tame 'em if you known how, and you've plenty of patience.'

'But what do you tame them *for*?'

'Hunting rabbits,' said Ben and laughed at Dan's puzzled face. 'They're the best hunters I know, better than a dog. Put 'em down a burrow and they'll go through every twist of it. Out come the rabbits and –' He made a sharp chopping movement with his hand.

'Oh,' said Dan doubtfully. 'I see. You mean they'll drive the rabbits out from underground for you?'

'That's right.'

76

'But what had happened to ours?'

Ben scowled at the fire. 'Some idiot tied its mouth up so it wouldn't kill underground and stay there; then he lost it so he left it to starve. And I'd like to get my hands on him. There's no call to treat a ferret that way.'

'But that's a terrible thing to do. Who'd want to do a thing like that?' Dan was horrified.

'There's all sorts'll keep ferrets. Keeper has them and some of the farmers have them as pets and some keep them for poaching.'

'Poaching!' Dan breathed.

'And there's bad and good poachers like any other business. A bad poacher will starve his ferret to make it hunt and tie its mouth to stop it killing. Do you know,' he said, shaking a forefinger at Dan, 'I've known some as sewed their mouths up with a needle and thread. And there's no need for it. Just get your ferret to know you, study it, handle it, feed it right, and it'll work right. Amateurs, that's what they are, just amateurs.'

He was as angry as he had been by the river, and Dan sat quiet and drank his tea, watching him over the rim of his mug. He was glad he wasn't the one who had done it.

'Won't he ever get over it and be tame again?' he asked at last.

'Of course he will,' Ben leant across and patted his knee. 'We'll manage it between us. You did all right today. Now give us a hand to carry the hutch out.'

Praise from Mr 'Uggett was a rare thing. It made Dan feel he could cope with anything, even taking a ferocious ferret. Proudly he took one end of the hutch and helped manoeuvre it through the kitchen door and out into a sheltered spot by the house wall, where, Mr 'Uggett explained, the ferret could see them come and go and get used to them. Dan squatted on his heels and peered in to make sure the movement had not frightened him, but the ferret, warm and full, was still curled in his bracken bed.

'What shall we call him?' asked Dan. 'Yellow, for his colour? Or shall we call him Ruby because of his eyes? They neither of them sound right really. Can you think of a name, Mr 'Uggett?'

'Well,' said Ben doubtfully. 'I don't go much for fancy names. I just call Dog, Dog.'

'That's easy then,' said Dan. 'We'll call him Ferret.' He leant closer to the wire. 'We're going to call you Ferret,' he said. 'And I'm Dan and the big one is Mr 'Uggett and we'll look after you very well so you mustn't be frightened and bite us.'

Ferret yawned wickedly, blinked his red eyes and went to sleep.

'It's a pity he can't understand me,' said Dan. 'Still,' he added hopefully, 'you never know; perhaps he does.'

'Don't depend on it,' said Ben dryly. 'You get hold of a pair of gloves. I reckon that's safer!'

They were both unwilling to move. The contrast between the ferret they had found and the ferret in the hutch gave them immense satisfaction and they were quite content just to sit in the sun and watch him sleep. The

repeated sound of a car horn in the lane startled them both.

'That's the farm van!' exclaimed Dan, leaping to his feet. 'Someone's come to fetch me. I didn't think it was as late as that.'

'It isn't,' said Ben. 'You'd best go and see what they want.'

Dan ran round the corner of the house and Ben followed more leisuredly. George was in the van, leaning across from the driving seat to talk to Dan who was hovering anxiously by the open gate.

'How be, Ben?' he called. 'Sorry to disturb you but we're a bit rushed. I need Dan early.'

'Trouble?' asked Ben, looking at Dan's worried face.

'No, not really. Mr Knott cut his hand oiling the mower. Had to go up the hospital and get it stitched. Stop him working for a bit so Dan'll have to take over. Lucky he's here, eh?' He grinned cheerfully.

'Hop in then, Dan. What you waiting for?'

'But Mr 'Uggett,' Dan edged closer, 'what about Ferret? You said you were too busy to look after him, and I may not be able to get here much 'til Uncle Jim's better.'

'Don't you fret yourself, I'll keep an eye on him,' said Ben calmly. 'Just you come when you can.'

'Well, if you're sure . . .' said Dan, climbing into the van.

'I'm sure.' Ben shut the door. 'Dan found a ferret down by the river,' he explained. 'He's keeping it here to save Mrs Knott the trouble; but,' and he stared hard at George, 'it's Dan's ferret, see.'

He watched the van to the bend in the land and then went slowly back up the path. He had time to take a hoe to the carrots before he had his bit of supper. There was a nice chop in the larder; if he cut the end off he could shred it up for the ferret tomorrow. He looked contentedly round the garden and went to fetch the hoe, but by the back door he hesitated and then took a quick look inside the hutch before moving on. The sight of the ferret pleased him. It was good to see the hutch in use again; like old times, very right and proper. He liked a nice ferret.

Chapter 9

LOOKING BACK afterwards, Dan was always amazed that someone else's cut finger made such a difference to him. But because of it things changed, and he changed too. He thought he had worked quite hard on the farm; now he realized that he had not really worked at all, he had just been playing at it. He had done things that were fun, he had taken his time, dawdling in the sun when he felt lazy and free to go off whenever he wanted to. They had said 'Thanks for helping,' and 'Well done,' but he had a shrewd suspicion it was because they had not really expected him to do anything at all. In fact they had been looking after him, entertaining him, giving him a holiday. Now they really needed him.

The first evening was not very different from any other. It was strange doing the milking without Uncle Jim, but he and George managed very well, though it took them a bit longer. At first he just brought the cows in and out, washing them down and feeding them as usual, but after a while George called him over.

'Here,' he said, 'you'd best give me a hand with this or we'll never get done. We're behind already.'

And he showed him how to fix the teat-cups to the cows and start milking. He was awkward at first and fumbled. It made the cows restless and he had to dodge a kick or two, take off the cups and start again, but it was easier than he had thought, though he had to leave finishing off to George.

'Must make sure they're milked out,' he explained. 'Or the yield will drop.'

With both of them at it they were a lot quicker, and when Pat came to see if they needed help, the last cows were already in the milking bays and George sent her back again.

'It's all right, Mrs Knott,' he said. 'You leave it to us. We don't want Mr Knott thinking we can't manage or he'll be trying to do it himself.'

'OK,' said Pat. She turned to go and then came back.

'George,' she said. 'We really must stop him until he's had the stitches out. They've put him on penicillin but the Doctor said he'd be lucky if it didn't get infected. It was much worse than I'd thought. Do you think you can cope?'

'We're not that busy. We'll manage,' said George.

'Of course we will,' said Dan.

They both looked at him. They had forgotten he was there. Auntie Pat smiled doubtfully and said, 'Well, thank you, Dan,' and, hurt that they had not counted on his help, he thought, 'She doesn't really think that I can do anything. She thinks it's just George and her.'

He watched her cross the yard, and then went angrily

back to work. 'All right, little Aunt,' he decided, 'I'll show you. We won't just manage, we'll do everything Uncle Jim would have done . . . just you wait and see.'

He didn't know how stormy he looked. George, stripping the last cow, ducked his head into her flank and grinned. He could tell from Dan's face what he was thinking. Well, if he wanted to prove his Aunt was wrong good luck to him, and he would help him on his way!

'Get the hose fixed up, Dan,' he called, and winked broadly at him.

'Women!' he said, and Dan winked back.

He was late for his tea. Instead of leaving as soon as he had hosed down the shed, he stayed to help George sterilize all the equipment and then took the cows down to the Home Field himself.

'I can manage them. Really!' he said. 'You go and get your tea. And George – see you in the morning.'

'Well . . .' said George doubtfully. 'Morning milking's awful early.'

'I won't oversleep.' Dan was determined. 'I'll be there,' and he was off to open the gate for the cows before George could argue.

He was hungry by the time he got back to the farm. There was no trace in the kitchen of the chaos of the afternoon but it was strange to see Uncle Jim sitting idle. He looked rather white, as though his hand hurt him, and he had a very impressive bandage.

'Crikey,' said Dan, 'they wrapped you up well.'

Uncle Jim insisted it was not as bad as it looked, just a damn nuisance and not worth so much fuss, but he could not cut up his meat or spread his bread and butter, so Dan decided that Auntie Pat was right. It was really bad and between them they must see he took care of it.

As soon as they had started tea Dan told them about the ferret. It was the most exciting thing that had ever happened to him, and not even Uncle Jim's accident could spoil it. He had wondered whether they would approve but he need not have worried, they were as pleased and interested as if they had found it themselves.

'It's fantastic,' said Uncle Jim. 'It's a chance in a thousand. You often hear of people losing ferrets but I've never heard of anyone finding one before.'

And Auntie Pat promised to find him an old pair of gloves as soon as she had finished tea.

'Though I'm glad you're keeping it at Mr Huggett's rather than here,' she admitted. 'It's very kind of Mr Huggett; are you sure he won't mind?'

'Oh he won't mind,' said Uncle Jim, and would not tell them why he was laughing.

Armed with his gloves and the promise of a regular supply of meat scraps, 'Raw,' said Uncle Jim, who seemed to know about ferrets, 'And not more than twice a week,' Dan slipped off early to bed. They thought the excitement had tired him. It had not, but he was determined not to oversleep. No one mentioned the morning milking, but he guessed that his Aunt meant to get up and do it. If he was to stop her he had to plan carefully.

He knew that normally Uncle Jim got up first, came down and put the kettle on, made them both a cup of tea, and then went out to the cow shed. So to stop Auntie Pat he would have to get up even earlier. When he was ready for bed he slipped into their bedroom. As he had hoped, their alarm clock was there, unwound but set for five o'clock, so five must be the time Uncle Jim got up. He checked it again to make sure, and then shutting the door very quietly, ran back to his room.

He had his own clock on his bedside table. Auntie Pat had put it there when he first came so that he would know the time if he woke in the night. He had never used the alarm on it before but now after a minute's thought he set the timing hand to half past four, carefully wound it up and tucked it under his pillow. That should muffle the sound so no one heard it but him, and surely an extra half hour would be time enough? He drew back the curtains, turned out the light and got into bed. Just to make quite sure he would wake he banged his head against the pillow, four hard bangs for the hours and one gentle one for the half, and then snuggled happily under the bed-clothes, confident that he had thought of everything.

He woke quietly and lay blinking sleepily at the grey ceiling, trying to trace the source of the strange ticking sound beneath his right ear. Without warning it changed to a muted buzz. The alarm clock! Wide awake now he whipped over on to his stomach and dragged the clock under the bedclothes, fumbling for the button to switch it off. Then he sat up, listening intently. The house was quiet.

He dressed quickly, crept downstairs and let himself into the kitchen. The cat leapt from a chair and purred round his legs as he lifted the warm kettle from the back of the stove and put it to boil. It was nice to be welcomed, so he gave it a saucer of milk, and then helped himself to a thick slice of bread and butter. He made the tea and drank his own, thinking that it seemed much hotter and sweeter than it usually did at breakfast. It filled the hollow inside him very satisfactorily.

'Now for the tricky bit,' he thought, putting two mugs of tea on a tray and going back upstairs. They were still asleep, curled round each other in the big bed like, he grinned suddenly, like two kittens. He almost expected them to purr. It seemed a shame to wake them, and he was not sure how to do it with his hands full. He was looking round for somewhere to put the tray when the alarm shrilled loudly, the bedclothes heaved and his Aunt struggled over and switched it off.

'Oh no,' she muttered, and gave an enormous yawn.

'Good morning, Auntie Pat,' said Dan brightly and pushed a mug of tea into her hands.

She stared at him blankly, blinking like a rumpled owl.

'Good God!' she said, 'What on earth are you doing?'

'The milking, of course,' he said firmly. 'Now don't rush to get up, there's plenty of time before breakfast. I hope the tea's all right, and here's some for Uncle Jim.'

He put the second mug down by the bed and made rapidly for the door.

'Dan, come back here!' she said, desperately trying to collect her thoughts. 'It's much too early for you to be up. I'm doing the milking.'

'No, you're not. George is expecting me, it's all arranged. You're cooking the breakfast like you always do. So please, Auntie Pat, drink your tea and leave the milking to me.'

'But . . .' she began.

A smothered laugh came from beneath the bedclothes.

'Give up, woman, don't you know when you're beaten?' said Uncle Jim. 'Off with you, Dan!'

'But . . .' she tried again.

'Thanks, Uncle Jim,' Dan said quickly, and was through the door before she could argue.

He went out into a magic world, pearl grey and tumbling with bird song. The mist lay like water in the hollows; the cows waded through it to the gate, their breath steaming. Above the hills to the east the sky was transparent with light and the morning wind washed cold against his cheeks. He had never seen the day begin before. He wanted to stay and watch it, but the cows were moving steadily towards the yard, their udders heavy with the night's milk. It would not be fair to keep them waiting and anyway George would soon be here. There was work to do.

And work he did. All day. George knew what had to be done and quietly got on with it, making sure Dan shared the jobs with him, never fobbing him off with something easy. He realized that Dan was on his mettle and was secretly amused by it. It would not do him any harm to find out what farming was really like.

Jim had come to the same conclusion.

'Leave him,' he said to Pat when she worried. 'Let him get on with it. George will look after him.'

He nursed his throbbing hand and watched from a distance.

Luckily it was a slack time. The ploughing, the sowing, the muckspreading were done, and the grass needed more time to grow before it was ready to cut for silage. But there was a long list of jobs which they had planned to do now so that they would not be overstretched when silage and haymaking started. Buildings, fences, gates, machinery; they all needed to be checked and any faults repaired.

So Dan found himself with a bucket and a brush, slapping whitewash on the outbuildings while George repaired a broken gutter; he mixed cement and fixed the loose tiles on the pigsty roof, which he could reach, while George, on a ladder, mended the high roof of the old barn. He fed calves and pigs and mucked out the pens so that George was free to overhaul the tractor, the baler, and the mower. Together they took the tractor and inspected fences and drainage ditches, and every day saw to the young stock out at grass because, George explained, accidents could happen, you had to make sure they were all right; and twice every day there was the milking.

To begin with Dan was so tired that he ached all over, nearly fell asleep during tea, and rolled into bed dreading the moment when the alarm would ring. He dragged himself up in the morning fighting waves of sleep, and only a grim determination not to be beaten stopped him from begging Auntie Pat to get up, just once, and do the milking instead of him.

Every day he snatched half an hour to go down to Ben 'Uggett's. The ferret was beginning to know him and come to the door of the hutch when he fed it instead of chittering at him from the farthest corner. But it still tried to bite when he picked it up and he was too tired and rushed to be patient and despaired of ever taming it.

'It'll come,' said Ben, unhurried as always; and made him tea, and sat him down near the warm stove. It was a relief just to be quiet and twice he went to sleep with his drink untouched and Ben had to wake him when it was time to go.

'It's too much for him!' Pat protested. 'You'll have to stop him, Jim. He'll make himself ill.'

But Jim shook his head.

'Leave him,' he said. 'He needs to do it. He'll be all right.'

Imperceptibly Dan adjusted to the long hard days. He was still glad when evening came, but he was not so tired that it hurt, and though getting up was still an effort, he found he enjoyed being the only one awake in the grey stillness of early morning. He ate enormous meals and slept without stirring. The blisters on his hands broke and then hardened, his skin lost the last trace of its pallor. He reported back to Uncle Jim on the condition of the stock, the state of the hedges and gates, the milk yield; and as Jim's hand healed allowing him to drive round and see things for himself, the reports changed to discussions.

At some point in that hectic two weeks he came, almost without realizing it, to an irrevocable decision. This was how he wanted to spend his life. When he was grown and free to choose for himself at last, he was going to be a farmer.

Chapter 10

THE DISTRICT nurse came every day, and then every other day to dress Jim's hand. The stitches were taken out, and then he was back at work with only a light bandage and fingerstall to keep the healing skin clean and dry. Dan still got up for the milking. He seemed to have got into the habit of waking up so it seemed a waste to stay in bed, and he had grown to love the early morning. Milking was less rushed now with three of them to do it and there was more time to look round, to stop and listen to the birds marking the boundary of their territory with song, or examine the intricate pattern of the cobwebs on the grass only visible while the dew was on them. Sometimes, moving quietly behind the cows, he saw the fox crossing the field on its way back to the wood, and once he saw a weasel.

'It was just like Ferret,' he told Ben. 'Only brown with a white shirt front.' And described how it had played hide and seek with him all the way down the hedge, peering out at him through the gaps in the twisted roots.

'Ar, they're curious little beggars,' said Ben. 'Pretty too, but cruel.'

He had more time to spend with Ben now that things were normal again, and was amazed at the way Ferret was responding to the extra handling. There was no doubt now that he knew him, and at times he could be almost affectionate, though Ben said dourly that it was cupboard love. Ben taught him to whistle through a piece of grass, held flat between his thumbs, and insisted that he always did it before he fed Ferret. Soon even if he was fast asleep it woke him and brought him to the front of his cage, and when Dan lifted him out he would run up his arm and across his shoulders to sit with his forepaws on Dan's head, watching and listening. He liked to burrow down inside his shirt too, and would lie quietly, curled round Dan's waist in the dark. Dan carried him there when he and Ben went out walking, for his pockets were too small and he was afraid of losing him.

'Chances are he'd come when you whistle,' said Ben. 'But it's best not to risk it. Anyway no one can see him inside your shirt. Keep the ferret hidden and wear clothes that help to hide you. Walk silently and don't talk unless you have to. Learn to stand still and keep under cover. Learn to use your eyes.'

It was second nature to Ben, and Dan, becoming more aware of his surroundings, also grew more aware of the man who was teaching him. Knowing how hard he found it all, he realized that Ben must have disciplined himself for years. Someone like Ben did not do that for fun, thought Dan, or because he wanted to see if the grass was still growing! That was the sort of explanation you gave to a child.

'And I'm not a child,' thought Dan. 'I've been doing a man's work for Uncle Jim, and I don't think Mr 'Uggett thinks I'm a child now, either.'

Anyway, Dan decided, he would have to risk it because he had come to a conclusion about Mr 'Uggett and he wanted to know if it was right. The only way to find out was to ask him.

He chose the moment with care; he was learning to be tactful. They had worked hard in the garden and were sitting on the bench in the sun with their afternoon mugs of tea. Ferret was running restlessly to and fro across his cage. It was too good a chance to miss.

'I think Ferret needs some exercise,' said Dan. 'Don't you?'

There was no response.

'Work perhaps?'

'Maybe,' said Ben, and drank his tea.

'Blast!' thought Dan. 'This is no good. There's nothing else for it. I shall have to ask him straight out.'

'I thought,' he said, 'you might be able to help. Working Ferret, I mean.'

'What makes you think that?' Ben was looking straight at him now and it was not encouraging or comfortable. But it was too late to back out. Flushing, he met the old man's stare.

'Mr 'Uggett,' he said, 'I haven't told anyone what we do. Not anyone. Not even Uncle Jim. I haven't talked at all, but I can't help thinking to myself. Mr 'Uggett, you are a poacher, aren't you?'

There was a long and terrifying silence. Dan could feel his heart thumping but he did not drop his eyes. Ben's face was stern, and his voice when he spoke was hard.

'That's not a name I like to be named,' he said, 'though some call me by it. Them as don't know the rights of it. Time was I deserved it, but not now.'

Dan sat there wishing he had said nothing; and then gradually Ben's face softened and he smiled.

'There now,' he said. 'I won't bite. And you're bound to think your thoughts.' He chuckled suddenly. 'Tell the truth, I wonder you haven't asked before, you with your questions.'

Dan grinned back.

'But I didn't, did I?' he said triumphantly. 'Maybe I'm learning. Though,' he added wistfully, 'I've wanted to ever since you took me to Big House.'

Ben considered him for a moment and then nodded as though he had come to a decision.

'Ah,' he said. 'You've learnt a lot of things, and keeping a still tongue's one of 'em. Reckon it's time you learnt the truth of this, but keep it to yourself mind. They tell tales of me down the village, some of them true and most not, but it keeps them happy. Those that do know, say nothing, and that's how I like it.'

'Well you can trust me too, Mr 'Uggett,' said Dan solemnly. 'I promise I won't say a word.'

Talk did not come easy to Ben. It was the bare bones of a story Dan heard that afternoon, but he decided he preferred it like that. He could fill in the details from his own imagination, and if he did not get them quite right, what did it matter? It was still a better story than any he had read.

It began years ago when Ben was a boy. He was the oldest of six children. His father was a farm labourer, they lived in a tied cottage on the other side of the village, and life was a struggle. Wages were low and there was always a new baby in the big wicker basket by the fire; and although not much more than a baby himself, he had to mind the younger ones.

'But it got worse when the war came,' he said. 'And I was older then, old enough to mind.'

He was seven when the Great War began, and nearly eleven when his father came home at the end of it, shell-shocked and sick and incapable of work. They lost the tied cottage. The three eldest children went out to work, stone-picking, bird-scaring, anything to earn a few pence. Mother took in washing and they moved to a damp little house on the outskirts of Banford.

'One of a row,' said Ben. 'Not fit for a rat. They've pulled them down now. Our mother was always tired and Dad coughing his lungs out. I used to dream of food.'

It was because they were all so hungry that he poached his first rabbit. He used to see it every evening when he stumbled back from work in the half light; a big fat buck feeding by the hedge. He stole some wire, set a snare and went every day to see if he had caught it. It took him over a week.

'I wasn't doing it right, see? There's a knack to it, and there was no one to show me. Respectable our Dad had been, always, but I soon learnt the way of it.'

You learn fast when you are hungry, Dan decided. It was easy for him to picture young Ben, the same age as he was now, slipping across the fields and down the hedgerows before dawn to reset his snares and retrieve the night's haul. Necessity taught him how to weight a snare so that it killed clean. A screaming kicking rabbit drew attention and that was dangerous. And necessity taught him to recognize the track in the grass which marked the run of rabbit or hare, the best place to set for them and how to camouflage his handiwork, for empty snares meant empty bellies.

'Our mother didn't like it,' said Ben. 'But she couldn't say no. She knew Dad wouldn't work again and she couldn't earn enough for us all. Times were bad for everyone. Half the town was out of work.'

Soon Ben was catching more than they ate, and dis-covered that he could sell what was left.

'And that was it,' he said. 'I didn't bother much with steady work after that.'

A discreet word here and there and he found plenty of customers, and as he gained in experience he grew more daring and tried other methods. Listening, Dan went with him down the dark tracks, netting driven hares as they ran under the field gates; and crawled on his belly through the rushes by the river to gaff salmon in the deep pools below the falls, one ear cocked for the water bailiff. Rabbits were bread and butter, but salmon, hare and pheasant bought the jam. By the time he was fourteen Ben was tough and wiry and wild as they come. His father was dead, and the local landowners knew perfectly well who kept the family in shoes and clothes and food. But Ben was cunning and they could not catch him.

'But our mother still took in washing,' said Ben. 'If I could have earned enough honest like to stop her, I doubt I'd never have gone poaching. But I couldn't get a job with a decent wage. Men's wages were bad and I was only a boy. The house was full of steam all day, and nights she did the ironing. I still hate the smell of washing. And,' he admitted honestly, 'It gets hold of you, poaching. I enjoyed it.'

He liked the freedom and the running battle with the keepers. He was very skilful and proud of it, and too young to be discreet, so inevitably he ran into trouble. He had been systematically lifting pheasants from the Big House. Night after night he had scattered stolen corn for them until they came regularly for their feed.

'I don't like guns, you see,' he explained to Dan. 'And this way is safer. When I knew I could sell them I soaked the corn in whisky. It makes them drunk, and there they are, lying on the ground waiting for you to pick 'em up. But that night the keepers was waiting too and they got me. Didn't stand a chance with me arms full of dead pheasants and the ones I didn't want lying drunk at me feet!'

They took him to the Squire and the Squire was shocked to discover that the desperate poacher his Head Keeper had told him about was a cold, defiant and frightened boy of fourteen. But the Squire was also very angry, so Ben was shut in an empty storeroom for the night and in the morning Mrs Huggett was sent for.

'I could have gone to prison, I suppose,' said Ben, 'but Squire and our Mother worked it out between them that it would be worse for me to have to do a steady job. And they were right too. The stable boys gave me hell, and so did the keeper. I've never been so miserable in my life.'

'Then why did you stay?' asked Dan.

'Didn't have no choice,' said Ben wryly. 'I lived at the Big House but Squire paid our Mother's rent, gave her my wages and kept an eye on things. She'd have lost all that if I'd run off, so there I was. But it worked out well. I was Under Keeper by the time I was twenty and when the old Keeper retired Squire gave me the job and the cottage for me and our mother to live in. Set a thief to catch a thief, Squire said, and maybe he was right. I was a good Gamekeeper, and our Mother got her garden.'

'But what went wrong?' asked Dan puzzled. 'Why aren't you the Keeper now?'

'Squire died,' said Ben bitterly. 'And those city folks came. There's an Agent runs the place now, and he put his own men in. He said I was too old. Mr Jones came as Keeper. I offered to lend him a hand, but he said he'd have me for trespass if he found me on his land.'

His voice grew fierce.

'But they couldn't take my cottage. Squire left me that for life. And I walk where I choose, and no one can stop me.'

Dan was overwhelmed by such a wave of anger and

97

loyalty that he could hardly speak. How could people be so blind? How could anyone think Mr 'Uggett was too old and treat him like that?

'That's terrible,' he said. 'Isn't there anything you can do?'

'Only one thing, Dan,' said Ben smiling. 'And I'm doing it.'

'You mean you're poaching again?'

'Now Dan, never call it poaching. Poaching is for profit. A little bit of harassment is what I'd call it.' His smile grew until his whole face was crinkled with amusement. 'Wouldn't do for Mr Jones to get careless, would it now? So now and then I give him a little something to worry about. That's all.'

So that was it, thought Dan. How very satisfactory, much better than anything he had imagined. He realized that he had been a bit worried in case Mr 'Uggett might be mixed up in something really illegal, but this was splendid; poaching but with right on your side. It was like a crusade.

'Oh Mr 'Uggett,' he said longingly, full of admiration. 'Can I help? Would you possibly let me?'

'You never know,' said Ben. 'We'll wait and see. I make no promises.'

And with that he had to be content.

Chapter 11

EVERY WEEK on a Tuesday, Dan got a letter from home. Usually it was his mother who wrote, though occasionally his father added a sentence or two at the end. They were nice letters full of news, and his mother obviously tried very hard to think of things that would interest him. She told him about the new curtains she had bought for the sitting-room, and that Tommy down the road had had a bike for his birthday. She told him that now it was warmer they had started to go swimming again. The golf club Dad belonged to had a swimming pool and Dan felt a momentary pang of envy because he enjoyed swimming, it was the only sport he was good at, and it really was a super pool. She told him all the things the twins had been doing and who she had met shopping or invited for coffee. She told him she missed him, and was glad to hear he was getting well so quickly, and she sent him her love; but neither she nor Dad ever mentioned school or seemed worried because he was missing so much time there. Which was odd, Dan thought, because before they had made an awful fuss if he was away for a single day. They must have decided that it just did not matter any more now that they knew he could not go to school with the twins . . . it was too late.

And so though he pounced on the letters when they came and read them eagerly, he dreaded them too. They reminded him of things he wanted to forget, and made him feel lost as though he had not got a home at all. He knew without having to think about it that he loved them all very much, but their world of shopping and new bicycles and swimming pools seemed so unreal compared with the world of the woods and the farm that he had discovered here. And the trouble was he did not belong here either; soon he would have to go back and he felt terribly guilty because he did not want to.

But except when the letters came he could pretend that this was home. So he read them and then pushed them away and tried to forget that the summer could not last for ever.

It was not difficult. He felt as though he had never really seen or smelt or listened before and he was surrounded by so much colour and light and sound that it seemed as if his senses were being stretched. Everything was green and growing, dappled with sunlight and cloud shadow, so many different greens he could not count them. The hedgebanks were splashed with yellow archangel and red campion and delicate Queen Anne's Lace, and the woods smelt of bluebells and crushed wild garlic and echoed with bird-song. Everywhere he went he heard the cuckoos calling, and now the swifts were gradually returning so that every day there were more of them to dive screaming round the house in the evening and swoop like minute black aeroplanes in and out of the big barn.

Above all there were his walks with Ben, which, he discovered with a shock, were and always had been carefully planned. They followed the familiar tracks which they had walked many times before, but now Ben stopped and showed him the purpose behind his apparently aimless wanderings. Hidden in the grass and under the brambles beside fallen logs and piles of brushwood were the Keeper's snares. Dan had begun to pride himself on being observant, but he had never noticed them. Ben's trained eye saw them all.

'That's a snare, isn't it?' Dan asked, the first time Ben parted the grass to show him the loop of thin wire staked under a hazel bush beside the unmistakable line of a run.

'It's meant to be,' said Ben scathingly. 'But it's a bad one.'

Dan could not see why. It was simply a long piece of wire with a loop on one end, supported on a notched stick, and with the tail of the wire tied to a peg driven into the ground about two feet away. Obviously if anything pushed into the noose the supporting stick would fall and the wire would pull tight. Which, thought Dan, is what is supposed to happen.

'What's wrong with it?' he asked puzzled.

'It won't kill clean,' said Ben. 'They can't get loose, the peg is in too firm. But you need weight to kill.'

'It's not your snare then?'

'Never! It's Mr Jones the Keeper's. Hush now, and watch how I do it.'

He stood for a moment looking carefully at the ground round about and then with a grunt of satisfaction moved to pick up a heavy stone. Very carefully he lifted the snare and its supporting stick to one side and pulled the anchor peg from the ground.

'Now then,' he said.

He untied the peg and replaced it with the stone. Then, using its weight to keep the wire taut, he angled the support stick over the run and slipped the wire into its notched end with the loop dangling free. He considered it for a moment and then pushed the stick carefully into the earth so that the loop hung a few inches above the ground.

'There,' he said. 'Any higher and it misses, any lower and it catches a foot. But measure it with your eye. Grass holds the scent if you touch it.'

He camouflaged the stone and trailing wire with twigs

and dead leaves and then moved silently on, beckoning Dan and Dog to follow. The whole complicated operation had only taken him a few minutes.

They found many more snares that day. Some of them Ben reset, weighting them like the first one, but some of them he just pulled up and hid in his big coat pockets.

Dan was bursting with questions which he did not ask, for Ben had a strict rule of no talking in the woods, and he did not need to be told that tampering with snares was a risky business. To be caught today would be disastrous. So he kept watch while Ben worked and thought happily that here was proof that Mr 'Uggett trusted him. Explanations would come later.

He did not have to wait long. As soon as they were back at the cottage with the kettle put to boil and the bundle of snares hidden behind a sack in the shed, Ben settled himself in his chair and said, with a pleased smile,

'There's a good day's work.'

'Mr 'Uggett,' said Dan boldly, for now there was no forbidden ground, 'please will you tell me what you were doing?'

'Well, it's like this, see. Old Jones, he's not a bad keeper but his ways aren't mine. All he cares about are his pheasants so he's out to get every stoat and weasel and fox he can. There's money in pheasants. But to my way of thinking there's more to Keeping than that.'

He leant forward, frowning with the effort of trying to explain.

'Of course you've got to keep the vermin down, and snaring is the best way. But if you're going to kill you must kill clean. And you mustn't kill too many. You've got to keep the balance, that's the important thing. You keep the balance and the woods will look after themselves.'

The kettle started to boil and he got up to make the tea.

'Take rabbits now,' he said, over his shoulder. 'Rabbits don't harm pheasants so Jones leaves them alone. We're overrun with them. The farmers complain but the warrens are on Estate land and Jones won't let the farmers in to catch 'em. He sets snares for the vermin but he sets bad snares and too many of 'em so I go round and puts things to rights. They were my woods for more than twenty years, and they'll stay my woods while I can still walk round them.' He turned with the teapot, and winked at Dan. 'Course Jones don't like it but he hasn't caught me yet. It's his own fault. He should do the job properly himself.'

In the process of helping Mr 'Uggett teach Mr Jones how to do the job properly, Dan's own knowledge grew. Animals, Ben explained to him, hunt and feed at dawn and dusk. A good keeper checks his traps every day for even the best set snares occasionally catch without killing and no one, said Ben, had the right to leave a creature to die slowly in fear and pain. Mr Jones often left his traps for several days. So Ben and Dan checked them for him.

'It's safe to do in daylight,' said Ben. 'It's no riskier than a walk if you're quick and quiet.'

'But,' said Dan, 'these are the walks we've always done. How did you manage when I first came with you? I didn't know the snares were there and you never touched them.'

'Oh,' said Ben casually. 'I just looked them over on the way and came back later.'

Dan was horrified. 'You mean you had to walk all that way a second time just because I was with you? Oh, Mr 'Uggett, you shouldn't have done that!'

'Get along with you,' said Ben embarrassed. 'I'm used to it.'

But it made Dan realize that this was not some kind of game. Annoying Mr Jones might be fun, and Mr 'Uggett would do it whenever he had the chance, but it was not

important. It was the woods and the creatures living in them that really mattered.

Sometimes the snares were empty, and then Ben was pleased for it meant Mr Jones had been round them.

'I've got enough to do setting them properly and seeing he don't put down too many,' he explained. 'And if he decides to put 'em somewhere different it takes time to find 'em.'

'But he must know what we're doing,' said Dan. 'Why doesn't he hide and try to catch us?'

Ben laughed. 'I expect he does,' he said. 'But he's not to know which way I'll go, and Dog would tell me in time if he was near. That's why we always walk up wind.'

'Oh,' said Dan. So that was why they sometimes went a very long way round. He had not noticed the wind.

'I'm not very good yet, am I?'

'You'll do,' said Ben.

Most days at least one of their snares had killed and then Ben insisted that they bury the corpse. They usually caught stoats or weasels and at first it upset Dan. The weasel he had seen in the hedge had been so beautiful with its shiny brown coat, and so like Ferret. Mr 'Uggett said it was necessary, so he must try not to mind, but he handled them gently as he loosed the wire and buried them. It was the least he could do.

Mr Jones had a nasty way with corpses. He spiked them in rows on the barbed wire fences, or hung them in bundles from the fence posts. It made Ben very angry.

'There's no call for it,' he said. 'They just rot there. It doesn't keep others away.'

So when they found them, they buried those too. The little sagging bundles of fur with flies clustered round their blind eyes made Dan's stomach heave, but he hooked them off the wire swallowing hard. After this, he thought furiously, he wouldn't mind how often he broke the law provided it hurt Mr Jones.

Back at the cottage Ben initiated him into the art of making and setting snares. It took a lot of practice. Each one was different depending on what you were trying to catch, from thin twine for a rabbit to heavy stranded wire for a fox.

'Don't ever snare for foxes though, Dan,' Ben warned. 'You can't kill 'em; you just catch their feet. If they snap the wire they'll die of blood poisoning. If they're still there you have to shoot 'em. Either way it's a messy business. They're nasty cruel varmints, I know, but they deserve better than that. Leave foxes for them that have guns.'

'Have you got a gun, Mr 'Uggett?' asked Dan.

'Ah,' said Ben. 'That'd be telling. You need licences for guns.'

'I see,' said Dan, quietly deciding that Mr 'Uggett did have a gun but did not have a licence; and concentrated on the peg he was whittling.

He had discovered that even snare pegs had to be specially made. Hazel wood made the best. It was resilient enough to take the strain without snapping; but each peg had to be just the right length and thickness, carefully cut

and notched and then rubbed with earth to hide the new white wood.

And when you had the right pegs and the right weight and the right strength of wire or twine for the noose, you still had to find the right place to set.

With Ferret tucked in his shirt he walked for miles with Ben, learning to tell the difference between a rabbit run and a badger's path, to recognize the rank smell of the fox which hangs round the roots of grass and brambles for hours, and if in doubt to look for hairs caught on the thorns or a pad mark in soft soil. He learnt that a feeding rabbit moves in zig-zags and the flattened grass will tell you where it lands and what direction it is going in. He learnt where the rabbit warrens were, and which fields the hares chose to feed in; and found the labyrinth of badger sets in the wooded slopes above the river, and learnt how to tell which were in use and which deserted by looking for fresh earth and discarded bedding and broken spiders' webs across the entrances.

He was completely absorbed by it all. Such minute attention to detail, such meticulous observation were things he had never experienced before. Ben was a demanding teacher and at first he panicked, afraid he would never remember everything. And then with a sense of elation he realized that he did remember; and even more important, that he was noticing things without having to remind himself to look for them. It was as though someone had drawn a curtain and for the first time he could look out on the world, see it properly and understand what he saw.

Chapter 12

IT WAS a flat grey day. The clouds stretched without a break, and although it was warm a persistent drizzle had fallen all morning. Dan knew summer could never be all sunshine and blue skies, but he disliked days like today. It was not too bad if it really poured, then you made the best of it and stayed in; but this misty dampness was neither one thing nor the other. You got wet without an anorak, you sweated with one on, and it was too muggy and close to stay indoors.

Auntie Pat was having an enormous bake because as soon as the weather improved it would be time to start making silage. It had to be done quickly while the grass was just right so all the farmers joined together and helped each other.

'Which means about five days of providing enormous teas for half a dozen hungry men,' she explained. 'And you wouldn't believe the amount of bread and cake they get through. Still, when they've finished here it's someone else's turn. And it's much better this way. If we all did it separately it would take too long and the grass would have gone past its best.'

He wandered out to the shed where George and Jim were wrestling with the cutter. The concrete storage areas were spotless, waiting for their new consignment of grass, the covering tarpaulins neatly stacked beside them, but the cutter was obviously causing problems.

'What's the matter with it?' asked Dan, propping himself in the doorway.

'God knows,' Jim said. He wiped a greasy hand across his forehead. 'Same thing happens every summer.'

'Can you mend it?' said Dan anxiously.

George grinned. 'Course we can,' he said. 'Give it a bang or two and tie it up with string. And if that don't work we swear at it. Grand flow of language Mr Knott has!'

'Get away!' Jim's voice came muffled from the depths of the cutter. 'The machinery on this farm runs on thumps and pieces of string. Oh, for some money or a kindly Bank Manager.'

There was a nasty clang and he straightened abruptly, took a deep breath and said.

'I think George is right. Off you go, Dan, we've got to the swearing stage!'

'All right,' said Dan cheerfully, 'If you think you might shock me I'll leave you to it. You'd better get it working now Auntie Pat's made all those cakes.' He made a face at them. 'If it isn't done when I get back you'd better let me have a swear. I've learnt some good ones from Mr 'Uggett!'

He was out and across the yard before they could reply.

Obviously, he decided, it was an afternoon when he'd

be better off at Ben's cottage. It was too wet for them to go out but there might be something he could do in the garden, or he could spend an hour quite happily with Ferret. He was pleased with Ferret. He was beautifully tame now and very healthy, with a sheen on his yellow coat and just the right amount of flesh on his bones. He knew Dan's voice and his whistle and when he was let out of his hutch would play round his feet as he sat by the back door, and follow him round the garden and into the kitchen. Mr 'Uggett said he should be proud of himself.

'That's how a good ferret should be,' he said. 'Tame as a dog; but it's not many as can train them to it. A born ferret handler, Dan, that's what you are. He's a credit to you.'

Dan was not sure which was the most satisfying, Mr 'Uggett's praise or Ferret's affection. All he wanted now was a chance to work him, but he would be patient and wait. Mr 'Uggett would tell him when Ferret was ready.

He was surprised when he got to the cottage to find Mr 'Uggett standing at the back door watching out for him, his old brown raincoat pulled over his shoulders.

'There you are, Dan,' he said. 'I was waiting for you. Another ten minutes and I'd have gone. Come on now, we've a job to do.'

'Coming!' said Dan, and moved to take Ferret out of the cage.

'Leave him be,' said Ben. 'We can't take him today. Put these in your shirt instead.'

He dug into his pocket and pulled out a bundle of snares. Without a word Dan took them and slipped them inside his shirt. They were cold against his skin and an awkward shape but his anorak was loose enough to hide them, and the pegs went neatly into his pocket. He felt a little shiver of excitement. Something, he thought, was undoubtedly up.

They went at their usual unhurried pace down the lane and into the wood, but as soon as they were out of sight of the road they walked as quickly as they dared. Fifteen minutes later they reached the far end of the wood, and Ben waited for Dan to join him.

'Now,' he said quietly. 'Take a good look round.'

They were higher here, and facing into the wind. The drizzle had thickened to misty rain and low clouds blotted out the hills on the other side of the valley. A fence edged the wood, wooden posts with pig netting and a single strand of barbed wire stretched along the top. Beyond it lay a sloping scrubby field with patches of close cropped turf interspersed with clumps of coarse grass and gorse bushes in full flower, shining yellow through the mist like trapped sunlight. In the distance Dan could just see the huddled buildings of a farm, and the line of telegraph poles which marked a road.

Puzzled, he turned to Ben.

'What am I looking for?' he asked.

'Anything, everything,' said Ben. 'There's been sheep in the field for weeks so I've not been near it. You can't mix sheep and snares. But it's alive with rabbits. And it's a dirty day, no one much about. I thought you could put what you've learnt into practice.'

'Me!' exploded Dan.

'Ssh!' hissed Ben fiercely. 'Keep your voice down,' and stood a moment listening intently. Then he turned back to Dan.

'Go on,' he said. 'You can do it. No one will think anything of it if they see a lad walking across the field. But it's an estate farm and they know me. That's why I waited for you.'

Mr 'Uggett was right. The field was clearly visible from the farm and he would be recognized easily. But no one knew Dan. And anyway who would be suspicious of a bored boy on a wet afternoon? Dan had to admit that Mr 'Uggett knew what he was doing. And, he realized suddenly, Mr 'Uggett was right about something else. He had said that Dan could do it and he could; he knew he could and he was going to prove it.

'All right,' he said, and immediately felt horribly frightened. If he did not go at once he knew he could not go at all. But Mr 'Uggett seemed to understand.

'Quick then,' he said. 'Dog and me'll wait here. Don't set more than six. Choose your places as you walk across, set on the way back. If you hear me whistle lie low. Off with you now.' One foot in the pig netting, a heave, and he was over the fence. The field seemed very big, and very exposed. He could feel his heart banging, and fear and excitement tightened his muscles. He did not dare look towards the farm; he must appear unhurried, as though he were there by chance.

The first few yards were agony. He did not notice a thing. Head down and shoulders hunched he just walked doggedly forward fighting the longing to run for the wood. And then gradually he relaxed. The sheep had cropped the grass close and it was springy under his feet. There were signs of rabbits everywhere; patches of bare earth, stamping grounds Mr 'Uggett called them, covered with droppings; and where the clumps of longer grass and furze gave cover he could see the marks of the runs and the runnels leading into the safe heart of the bushes. Concentration conquered fear and he zig-zagged apparently aimlessly across the field, every sense alert.

There he would set, between those tufts of grass, and there in the lee of the gorse bush, and there where those clumps grew close together with a run leading through them. By the time he had reached the far hedge he knew where his six snares would go.

He leant on the gate and stared across the next field as though he were trying to decide whether he should go on. At least he hoped that was what it would look like if anyone were watching. Then he turned his back on the gate and looked carefully round. A tractor was moving away from the farm, he could just see its roof going steadily along the road. No one else in sight. He looked at the place where he had left Mr 'Uggett and Dog but he could not see them. The only movement was the wind stirring the branches of the trees.

'Now,' he thought, 'I must do it now.' And forced himself away from the gate and back on to the exposed slope of the field.

Wherever it was possible he kept the gorse bushes between himself and the farm, and the places where he had chosen to set were all hidden from anyone looking up the hill. The first snare took him a long time. His hands were shaking so badly that he could not get the tethering pin to hold firm and for a moment he panicked, afraid that he would make a mess of it. Then he steadied himself. He could not see Mr 'Uggett, but sure as eggs Mr 'Uggett could see him. He just had to do it properly.

The pin went home. The snare hung at just the right angle and height. He breathed a sigh of relief and moved quietly on. The rain dripped down his neck and the gorse scratched him; but it smelt hot and sweet, his hands had stopped shaking and his snares were perfect, dropping into place as neat as peas in a pod. Triumphantly he climbed the fence and slipped silently back among the trees.

They were waiting for him where he had left them. Dog thumped his tail and Mr 'Uggett was smiling.

'Well done,' he said. 'To the manner born!'

Dan felt as though he had conquered Everest.

But by the time he got back to the cottage some of his excitement had drained away. He was very chilly and very wet and had begun to realize that there were difficulties ahead. What could he say to Auntie Pat to explain the state of his clothes? She was bound to realize that he and Mr 'Uggett did not normally go out in the rain. And the snares. He would have to go back and see if he had caught anything. When would he go? Setting was all right but he did not like the idea of walking across that field with a dead rabbit dangling from each hand. And suppose someone found the snares and remembered seeing him? The man on the tractor maybe? To the manner born Mr 'Uggett had said, but it was not true. He was just a coward.

'Oh Lord,' he thought, and took refuge with Ferret, taking longer than he needed to clean his cage and change the bedding so he would not have to go and face Mr 'Uggett.

He need not have worried. Ben came and fetched him and Ferret indoors, hung Dan's anorak and trousers to

dry by the stove, pushed a mug of tea into his hands and sat down. Ferret perched blinking redly on his shoulder and then curled round his neck and went to sleep.

'Now,' said Ben, 'listen carefully.' He nodded towards the stove. 'That lot will be near dry by the time you go home, so there's no need to worry your Aunt as to why you got wet. But there's those snares to empty. You'll give me a hand?'

'Oh yes,' said Dan. 'If I can.'

'Well, it can't be done in daylight. Would they miss you from the morning milking?'

Dan shook his head.

'I don't think so. I'm always up but sometimes I go for a walk instead of helping.'

'Good,' said Ben. He thought for a moment. 'Come straight here then as soon as it's light. Not down the lane. Come the back way over the fields. I'll be waiting for you. The door will be open; come straight in. There shouldn't be anyone about but it's best to be careful.'

'All right,' said Dan. 'What shall I do,' he added hesitantly, 'if Uncle Jim wants me or asks questions?'

Ben chuckled. 'Don't you worry about that,' he said.

'Just tell your Uncle Jim that Ben needs you. He'll understand.'

'Oh,' said Dan blankly and then smiled.

'Oh!' he said again, beginning to understand himself. So Uncle Jim was in on the secret too, was he? That made things much easier.

The rain had stopped when he went down the lane. There were breaks in the clouds to the south-west and the wind had freshened. No one asked him questions, they were too busy making plans for tomorrow. The forecast was good, the cutter had responded to treatment, the wind was drying the grass and the men from the neighbouring farm had rung to say they would be coming in the morning. Dan went early to bed.

He was up at half light and out of the silent house before anyone else was stirring. It was misty and very still; even the cows were still, lying down chewing the cud, slowly turning their heads to watch him as he went past. He walked quickly keeping close to the hedges, for the grass was long and luscious and it would be terrible to damage it before it was cut. He was glad to see a light in the cottage and a wisp of smoke from the chimney. Mr 'Uggett was up then. He had been afraid he was too early.

'But you see,' he explained between gulps of hot tea, 'they're starting the silage today so everyone will be very busy. So if I could get back before they've finished milking it would be a help. Then they might just think I overslept.'

'Ah,' said Ben wisely. 'That's the way to do it. No call then for anyone to wonder. You'll be back in time, don't fret.'

The world was still asleep as they went down the lane. They moved fast for there was no one about to see them, only the birds rustling and twittering in the hedges, and they told no tales. The dawn chorus flooded round them as they went through the wood and when they came to

117

the furze bank the grey of the sky was touched with blue
and pink, and colour was gradually seeping back into the
woods and fields.

'Sun's up,' said Ben. 'Must be five o'clock. Just right.'

'Why?' asked Dan.

'Because anyone down in the farm is in the kitchen
making tea and getting ready for the milking. They're too
busy to look up here.'

'Oh,' said Dan. It was obvious if you thought about it
and it made him feel a lot safer.

'Do you think I've caught anything?' he asked, suddenly
breathless with excitement, and not sure which would be
worse; empty snares to prove his incompetence, or a
plethora of dead rabbits.

Ben grinned at him, remembering his own first snare.

'Let's look!' he said.

They kept to the trees until they came to the far hedge
where Dan had stopped to lean on the gate; and looked
carefully round before they climbed the fence. A small
flock of pigeons flew arrow-straight across the valley and
strands of mist were drifting up from the trees. Nothing
else moved.

'Right,' said Ben. 'Keep low behind the furze and move
fast. Lift the snares and hide 'em. I'll deal with the catch.'

'OK,' said Dan, and made for the nearest clump of
gorse.

The first snare was empty, and the last; and one was
broken, the grass round it scuffed and torn.

'Hare,' said Ben briefly when he saw it. 'Kicked free,
weight was too light.'

But the other three had killed.

Dan was very quiet on the way back. The rabbits were
hidden, pushed deep out of sight in Mr 'Uggett's poacher's
pocket, with hardly a bulge to show that they were there.
But they were. He had taken the wire from their necks

and seen their glazed eyes. He had felt the limp weight of their bodies and the softness of their fur. They had been so very dead. He had not realized that he would mind and feel guilty. They would still be alive if he had not set the snares, and he did not want to see them again.

He stopped at the door of the cottage and caught at Mr 'Uggett's sleeve.

'Please!' he said desperately, and stopped. He felt stupid and he did not know what to say. Mr 'Uggett would laugh at him and think he was a baby not fit to help him. He would never take him out with him again. Why, oh why couldn't he be more sensible?

But it was no good. Mr 'Uggett was standing there, waiting for him to speak, wondering why he would not go indoors. Even if it ruined everything he would have to explain.

'I don't think I like killing things!' he blurted and stared blindly at the toes of his boots.

'Don't you, Dan?' Ben's voice was quietly unsurprised. 'I'm glad to hear it. I don't like it myself.'

Startled, Dan looked up.

'It's a funny thing, knowing how to kill,' the old man's voice went gently on. 'It's been part of my job, see, so I've had to think about it. There's some as do it for fun; they enjoy it and don't know when to stop. But you're like me, Dan. Every blessed time you'll catch yourself thinking "That's dead because of me!" and that's how it should be. That way you only take what's needful.'

He put a comforting arm round Dan's shoulders and drew him into the kitchen.

'Don't fret now,' he said. 'You set good snares and killed 'em quicker than a fox would, or a stoat. You've a skill to be proud of, and I know now you'll take care how you use it.'

Before Dan could stop him he delved into his pocket and laid the three rabbits on the table.

'Look at 'em, Dan,' he said briskly. 'They're big 'uns, these are. There's some good meat there for hungry stomachs.'

Dan looked and suddenly felt better. They *were* big rabbits; they were super rabbits. He could not help being pleased.

'Hey, Mr 'Uggett! What are we going to do with them?' he asked.

'Well,' said Mr Huggett. 'There's one for me.' He moved it to one side. 'And there's one for a young couple I know down the village who can't make ends meet.' He put that one with the first, and then fetched some newspaper from the cupboard, laid it on the table and wrapped up the third rabbit.

'And there's one for you,' he said and gave it to Dan.

'But I can't just walk in with it,' protested Dan. 'What would everyone say?'

'Course you can't,' said Ben laughing. 'Hide it in your

anorak till you get home, and then put it on the shelf in the back porch when no one's looking. You won't have to say anything. It'll be all right. Off with you now, and mind how you go!'

All the way back Dan worried. Suppose someone caught him? What on earth would he do? And someone on the farm was bound to see him. But the yard was deserted when he arrived and the sounds from the cow shed told him milking was well under way. The kitchen door was shut and the radio was on so no one saw or heard him slip into the porch and deposit the rabbit with a sigh of relief on the high shelf by the back door.

'Someone has sent us a present, Jim,' Auntie Pat said when they came in for breakfast. 'A nice fat buck rabbit.' She sounded pleased but surprised. 'It was in the porch. Do you know anything about it?'

'Me?' said Jim. 'Nothing to do with me.'

He looked across the table. Opposite him Dan was steadily eating bacon and egg, his eyes firmly fixed on his plate.

'If I were you, love,' Jim went on, 'I'd accept it and be grateful. But I wouldn't ask questions. Don't you agree, Dan?'

'Oh yes,' said Dan without looking up. 'Yes, I'm sure that would be best,' and quickly took another mouthful. Questions would be very awkward.

The day passed in a haze of sunshine, full of the smell of cut grass and tractor fumes, and the voices of men shouting above the noise of the cutter. Dan worked in the yard unloading the wagons as they were brought in, and layering the grass in the silos. By evening he was so tired he was nearly asleep on his feet.

'It's been quite a day,' he thought as he and Uncle Jim made for the back door. Just outside they both stopped and sniffed hungrily. A beautiful savoury smell was drifting out of the kitchen, the smell of onions and herbs and rich gravy. They sniffed again and looked at each other with complete understanding.

'Thank you, Dan,' said Uncle Jim, and winked at him.

There was rabbit stew for supper.

Chapter 13

JIM AND Dan had a private understanding. Nothing was ever said, in fact it made Dan giggle because he could not help picturing them as two cartoon figures with little balloons growing out of the tops of their heads and 'I know that you know that I know that you know!' written on them. But it was a helpful understanding. The rabbit stew had been super. Dan knew that more would be welcome and Uncle Jim not only made it easier for him to spend more time with Mr 'Uggett, he actually encouraged him. In fact it was through Uncle Jim that he began to work Ferret.

He did not realize at first what Uncle Jim was suggesting. It was just a casual message for Mr 'Uggett, and he went to the cottage to deliver it without suspecting that it had a double meaning.

'It's about some hedging,' he explained to Ben. 'Uncle Jim said that now we've got most of the silage cut he would be very grateful if you could spare him some time. He wants the hedges tidied up before the grass grows again, and he and George are still very busy. He said perhaps I could give you a hand, and if you can manage it could you start at the Long Meadow. And he said if you weren't sure where that was, it's the field next to the one where the rabbits are eating his turnips.'

Ben leant back on his chair and roared with laughter, stopped, saw Dan's indignant stare and laughed again.

'What's so funny?' said Dan. 'What have I said? I'm sure I've got the message right.'

'Oh yes, you've got it right,' gasped Ben, wiping his eyes. 'My, he's a caution, that uncle of yours. He was a little devil at your age, and I doubt he's changed by the sound of it.'

'You might explain,' said Dan. 'I give you a perfectly simple message and all you do is laugh. What am I going to say to Uncle Jim?'

'Tell him I'll do his hedging for him,' he said, still chuckling.

Mr 'Uggett was teasing him, and Dan knew it.

'No,' he said firmly. 'I'm not carrying any more messages until I know what's going on.' He plonked himself down on the edge of the table and glowered at Ben's mischievous face.

'There now, Dan,' said Ben relenting. 'It's only my bit of fun. You can work it out for yourself if you try, but I'll tell you. Rabbits, that's what it is. Rabbits eating his turnips.'

'But that's Uncle Jim's own land. He doesn't need us.'

'But the warren isn't on his land.'

Suddenly Dan understood. To catch warren rabbits you needed a ferret, plenty of time, and an excuse for hanging round; an excuse like hedging. He grinned happily, eyes alight as he began to appreciate what his uncle wanted. He had waited a long time for a chance like this.

'Ferret!' he said to Ben, and Ben smiled back and nodded.

'Just what we want for him,' he agreed. 'Come on now! We'll get things ready and tomorrow we'll go a-hedging, you and me.'

It was the first of a succession of similar days. The young turnips were not the only crops the rabbits were devastating. They had bred fast that year and were coming out at night and morning from the warrens to feed. The farm was overrun with them and it took more than one expedition to reduce their numbers.

Every morning Ben and Dan set off with billhook and drashing hook as camouflage, but deep in Ben's pockets was their collection of purse nets, and Dan carried Ferret safe hidden inside his shirt. They did the hedges. They cut them back and layered them and filled in the gaps. They piled the trimmings well inside the boundaries of Willow-garth and burnt them; and the smoke rose lazily upward, proof to anyone who cared to look of where they were and what they were doing.

But hedging, as Ben explained, is a useful kind of job. You can stretch it out to last all day, or hurry it on so that you have time to spare for other things; like rabbits.

So they always began by cutting a fair piece of the hedge. Then gradually Ben would slow the pace, taking a little longer each time he stopped to sharpen his hook, the stone moving rhythmically against the steel while his eyes noted the position of the rabbit holes and searched hedges and fields to make sure no one else was about. If Dog was restless, if the birds called a warning or a pigeon broke suddenly from the wood or altered its line of flight without reason, they went on with their work. Even on home ground Ben took no chances.

Towards the end of the morning they set their nets, pegging the edges firmly over the holes but leaving plenty of slack in the centre. They left one hole open for Ferret.

Even on the very first day Ben would not be hurried, working quietly on until Dan was nearly frantic with impatience. At last everything was ready. Ben gave a final look round but no one was in sight.

'All right,' he said to Dan. 'You can get him out now.'

Dan's hands were shaking as he unbuttoned his shirt and drew Ferret out into the light. The little animal caught his excitement and struggled to be free but Dan held him firmly, talking to him softly until he was still. Then he knelt down close to the open burrow, headed Ferret towards it and let him go.

For a moment Ferret stood there, looking round as though he could not understand why Dan had released him. Then he stiffened, his nose twitching. He had caught the scent of rabbit. He moved slowly forward sniffing delicately at the mouth of the burrow; and then suddenly he had gone, a flicker of white disappearing into the dark earth.

'And now we wait,' said Ben softly.

It takes time for a ferret to work a warren. It may look small with only a few holes but underneath the tunnels twist and turn, intricate as a spider's web. They sat in the sun and ate their sandwiches and all the time Dan's mind was underground with Ferret as he searched the dark maze; waiting . . . waiting . . .

Even so the first rabbit took him by surprise. Ben had gone back to his hedging but he heard the thump of the rabbit's feet and was there at the net before Dan realized what was happening. Dan saw him stoop and fish the rabbit out from the net, saw the quick sideways chop of his hand which killed it instantly, and then it had disappeared, bundled out of sight under a pile of hedge trimmings while they waited for the next one.

Four good rabbits Ferret raised for them that first day,

and a fifth that got away through a hole they had missed, hidden in the roots of the hedge. Once Ferret himself appeared under one of the nets, his sharp teeth gleaming, and blinked at them in the sudden light before he turned and went down again.

'That looks like the lot,' said Ben at last. 'You'd better get that Ferret out.'

'Right,' said Dan, trying to sound confident.

This was the real test. Would the weeks of handling, the patience, the training prove their worth? Or would he have to sit and wait for Ferret to come when he was ready?

He chose a blade of grass with care, wetted it and held it tight between his thumbs. He knelt by the burrow and blew as hard as he could, willing the shrill sound to echo through the warren and bring Ferret back.

And it worked. Within minutes they could see him peering out at them from a nearby hole. Dan ran and scooped him up, holding him tight for a moment before he fished in his pocket and brought out a plastic bag with a few scraps of meat in it. Ferret ate them carefully off the palm of his hand, yawned delicately and then, of his own accord, climbed on to Dan's shoulder and down inside his shirt. His coat was muddy and damp; it felt cold against Dan's skin, but he did not mind. Ferret had come back to him.

'I don't believe it!' he said jubilantly to Ben. 'I didn't really think he would once he'd got the scent of rabbit. I thought he'd go on hunting.'

'That's what most people think,' said Ben scathingly. '"You can't train a ferret," they say, so they never try. But I know you can, and you've just proved it.' He bent and picked up his drashing hook. 'Get those nets up, fast,' he said. 'You can work him again tomorrow.'

They were marvellous days. Each time he put Ferret

down a warren Dan felt the same breath-catching excitement, and the fact that Ferret chose to come back when he could have been free still seemed like a miracle. The hedging gave them an alibi so there was no need for silence and while they worked or waited, they talked. It was grand to eat lunch in the sun, back propped against a bank, or lie on the grass under the hot blue sky while the words flowed to and fro. Ben's stories were funny and sad, his wisdom immense. Dan absorbed it all.

In return, unwillingly at first and only because he felt he should contribute something, Dan tried to talk to Ben about his own family. Inevitably once he had begun he found he had to tell it all. Mr 'Uggett's questions were kind, he seemed really interested, and out it came. All the things he had been too hurt to talk about; how good the twins were at everything, how he had failed the exam and could not go to the school they had gone to; how he had let the family down and the other children had teased him, how Dad had wanted him to be a solicitor like him; even, he admitted it now, for the first time, his fear that they had left him so long at Willowgarth not because he had been ill, but because they were so ashamed of him they did not want him any more.

'I don't think they like me very much now,' he said miserably and rolled over, hiding his face in the grass, waiting for Mr 'Uggett to comfort him.

'I shouldn't think they do!' said Ben.

His voice was so kind it was a minute or two before Dan realized what he had said. When he did he shot upright staring at Ben in horrified amazement.

'You don't mean that!' he said. 'You can't!'

'Well,' said Ben, unmoved by Dan's shocked face. 'Seems to me it's only natural. There isn't a family living that doesn't have its ups and downs; and if you've been going round letting people wipe their boots on you, stands to reason your Mum and Dad won't like it. Come to that,' he added thoughtfully, 'our Mother found me a rare trial many a time. Shouldn't think she liked me much either. But remember this, Dan. It doesn't stop them loving you. There's a deal of difference between liking and loving.'

'Oh,' said Dan. This was a totally new view of the situation.

Ben let him think about it and then reached across and shook him gently.

'Now look here, Dan,' he said. 'I don't know nothing about exams and solicitors and what have you. I'd left school when I was your age, and I didn't bother with it much afore then, but I know you. And there isn't anyone I'd rather have by me when I've a job to do. Have a bit of pride, Dan. I reckon you've plenty to be proud of!'

Dan struggled for words.

'Thank you, Mr 'Uggett,' he said huskily at last. It was completely inadequate, but it was all he could manage.

Chapter 14

THE SILOS were full and the rich bitter smell of fermenting grass caught at Dan's throat whenever he crossed the yard, but the long hours of work went on. The fine weather had held, and the hay crop was ready for cutting. The men were out in the fields all day working until dusk fell and it was too dark for them to see; and Pat and Dan took on the yard work again just as they had in the Spring when Dan first came to the farm.

The Spring! Had the weeks really gone so quickly? thought Dan with shocked surprise. All the weeks between sowing and haymaking gone by without his realizing it? But it was true. It was high summer now, the bright greens of spring had darkened, the elder flower was fading in the hedges and there were small green hips as well as flowers on the trailing stems of the dog roses.

And so he worked with his aunt and he worked with the men, helping wherever he could; and all the time he watched and listened and asked questions. He had so much still to learn.

'Why does everyone rush so?' he asked Pat when for the third evening running Jim was still out with the cutter at nine o'clock. 'Surely he could do it in the morning?'

Wearily Pat shook her head.

'We can't risk it, Dan,' she said. 'We must get the hay in before the weather breaks. It's the winter feed for the herd, and it's worth a lot of money. If anything goes wrong with our hay crop we have to buy it in and we just can't afford to do it.'

And, he discovered, there were any number of things that could go wrong. It could rot or go mouldy if the weather caught you out or if it was not dried properly; but if you left it standing too long it might go musty, and if it was baled and stacked too early there was the risk of it growing so hot that it caught fire.

'But how do you know when it's ready?' he asked Uncle Jim. 'How can you be sure that you've chosen the right time?'

Jim picked up a handful of hay and rubbed it between his fingers.

'Dan,' he said, 'I really don't know. When it feels right and it smells right, then you bale it and bring it in. It's just experience, I suppose, and mistakes are so expensive you don't make them twice.'

Dan looked at him in despair.

'That's all right for someone like you, you've lived on a farm all your life, and you had your father to teach you. But what about me? I can't learn from experience.'

'Why not?' said Jim, and pointed to the grass at their feet. 'That needs another day's drying. Pick it up and smell it, and see what it feels like. When the next field is ready for bailing, do it again and try and remember the difference. That's experience!'

Carefully Dan did as he was told, marking the slight dampness and the sweet green scent.

'I'll remember,' he thought to himself. 'I mustn't forget anything, anything at all.'

He had to store it all away to help him in the months ahead. Growing up took a long time and he knew without being told that it would not be easy to hold on to his determination to be a farmer. It was strong now, but would it fade when the bustle of the milking shed, the back-breaking scratchy weight of the hay bales were only a memory? They were the exciting things like the chocolate on the outside of a biscuit. What he needed now was knowledge, the down-to-earth knowledge of why and how, because facts last longer than memories.

'Does anyone ever become a farmer if they're not a farmer's son?' he asked, trying hard to keep the longing out of his voice.

'Goodness, yes!' said Uncle Jim. 'Often. They go to an agricultural college when they leave school and then get a job on someone else's farm until they can afford to buy their own. That's the hardest part because farms cost a lot of money.'

'Does it matter what kind of school they go to?'

'Not a bit,' said Uncle Jim cheerfully. 'If people want something badly enough they usually manage to do it.'

That was as close as Dan got to talking about it. He did not want to say any more. When he had failed the examination everyone had known. No one was going to know about this ambition just in case he failed again; and if Uncle Jim had guessed, well, Uncle Jim was different. He would not say anything.

It was funny, he thought, he did not mind nearly so much about that exam now. Somehow it just did not seem very important. School was only school wherever you went; and if he had passed the exam Dad would have played merry Hamlet when he discovered that he was going to be a farmer, not a solicitor. So that was one battle less to fight. And if he had not been ill and failed he might never have come to the farm and then he might have lived all his life without realizing what he really wanted to do, all his life without ever being really happy.

'Uncle Jim,' he said, 'Life's very odd sometimes, isn't it?'

'Yes,' said Uncle Jim, 'It is. As Ben 'Uggett says: "Life's like an old ewe; you never know which way she's going to jump!"'

Dan grinned.

'He says that about the weather too,' he said.

'Sh!' said Jim. 'We don't talk about the weather. We'll just keep our fingers crossed.'

They had been lucky so far. The days were hot and sunny with a breeze to dry the hay. Every day after his tea Dan went to see Ben and Ferret and until late in the evening it was still light enough to tell the weeds from the plants and do a bit of gardening, or go for a walk across the fields with a snare or two. Dusk fell earlier in the woods but sometimes he was free in the afternoon to do Ben's 'rounds' with him, and the occasional rabbit still found its way on to the shelf in the back porch.

One evening he got back to the farm and found the kitchen and sitting-room empty. The lights were on, and the radio as usual was turned on low ready for the evening news, but there was no sign of his uncle and aunt.

He called up the stairs but there was no reply and the landing and bedrooms were in darkness. Where could they be? This was the time when they always came to the sitting-room or the kitchen to have a hot drink and relax after the day's work. It was an important time, especially when everyone was so busy and meals were rushed; often the only chance they had to talk and be peaceful together.

He stood uneasily in the middle of the kitchen wondering what to do. It was silly to worry but he had expected them to be there. They always were.

'Perhaps they went for a walk,' he said to the cat, and fetched the mugs from the dresser and the milk from the larder. It was no use making the drinks yet but he did not like the idea of just sitting in the empty house. It was better to be busy.

He was wondering what to do next when he heard someone running across the yard and Pat came quickly through the kitchen door. 'Hello,' said Dan. 'Where . . . ?'

But she interrupted him.

'Hang on,' she said. 'I'll explain in a minute.' And she ran straight through the kitchen into the sitting-room and picked up the phone. Dan stood in the doorway and watched her dial. What had happened? She looked anxious and was in such a hurry she had not stopped to take her boots off in the porch. Oh please! Not another accident.

Looking round she saw his white face and smiled at him.

'It's all right,' she said. 'I'm only ringing the vet. Can you put the milk on to warm, and then run upstairs and get Jim's anorak for me? Be as quick as you can.'

He heard her voice on the phone as he went upstairs, and the 'ting' as she replaced the receiver. He found the anorak and when he came downstairs she was already pouring coffee into a large thermos flask.

'What's wrong, Auntie Pat?' he asked.

'It's one of the heifers. She's started to calve rather early and she's making heavy weather of it. Jim wants the vet to see her to make sure nothing goes wrong. She's one of the best of our young ones. We don't want to lose her. Jim's worried.'

'Is there anything I can do?'

She smiled kindly but shook her head.

'There's not much anyone can do at the moment. We'll just have to hope for the best. I'll stay here to meet the vet, but Jim will stop with the heifer.'

She screwed the top on to the flask and reached for the anorak.

'I'll just take these out to him,' she said. 'If I were you I'd make a drink and get off to bed. There's no need for you to stay up as well.'

'But I'd like to,' said Dan quickly. 'Let me take those to Uncle Jim and I'll take another mug and have my drink out there with him. There might be something I can do.'

'All right,' she said. 'But don't get too tired.'

'Tired!' thought Dan indignantly as he struggled into his gumboots and anorak. Did she really think he was going to go quietly off to bed when a calf was being born and the vet was coming? Not likely!

Someone had turned the outside lamp on since he came home, and there was a light showing through the open door of the byre next to the milking shed, but even so the yard seemed dark after the bright kitchen. He picked his way across the uneven surface, carrying the slippery thermos very carefully, and stopped outside the door of the byre.

'Uncle Jim,' he called softly, 'I've brought your anorak.'

'Is that you, Dan?' His Uncle's voice was equally low. 'Bring it here will you, but go quietly. We don't want to frighten the poor girl.'

The heifer was in one of the end pens close to the light. Even to Dan's inexperienced eye she looked distressed, moving restlessly from foot to foot, with her head low and her breath coming noisily. Moving slowly so he would not startle her he put the thermos and mugs on the floor and sat down on one of the straw bales piled against the wall.

'What's gone wrong, Uncle Jim?' he asked.

'It's hard to say.' Jim came and sat beside him, shrugging gratefully into his anorak. It was a clear night and the byre was cold.

'I should have checked her this afternoon but I wanted to finish the Five Acre. I went back to it after tea and forgot about her. Stupid thing to do. She's not due for several days but even so I should have looked her over. She's been calving for some time; the calf should have come by now but something's holding it up.'

As they watched, her head went down, her back hunched and the muscles along her sides bunched and moved under the skin. Her breath came out hard as though she was groaning.

'It's hurting her, isn't it?' said Dan, feeling his own stomach muscles knotting in sympathy. 'And look! Under her tail!' His voice grew sharp. 'She's bleeding!'

The root of her tail was lifted stiffly and below it he could see the flesh dark red and swollen like a sponge; and a thick string of slime and blood hung down between her back legs.

'It's all right, Dan,' Jim put a reassuring hand on his shoulder. 'It's not as bad as it looks. That happens with any calving. It's her vulva that's swollen. It's got to grow bigger to let the calf through, and there's bound to be a little blood and some pain too. All her muscles are contracting to push the calf out, like a very bad cramp, and because the calf isn't moving it hurts and she doesn't understand what's happening.'

He paused and looked at Dan doubtfully.

'Are you sure you want to stay?' he asked. 'Don't if it's going to upset you.'

For a moment Dan was tempted. The kitchen was warm and bright, no blood or pain there. He could go back and in the morning there would be a new calf to make a fuss over; and if calf or cow died he would not have seen it happen. It would be easier that way, but he shook his head firmly.

'No,' he said. 'I'd rather stay.'

'Good,' said Jim, and smiled approvingly. 'Let's have that coffee then while we wait for the vet. There won't be time once he comes.'

The coffee was hot and comforting. They drank it sitting on the bales of straw, talking quietly and watching the heifer. The contractions hunched her back at regular intervals, and she was obviously very tired. It seemed a long time before they heard a car drive into the yard, the slam of the door and Pat's welcoming voice.

The vet was a big man, dark, cheerful and competent.

'Shame on you, Jim,' he said briskly as he came through the door. 'Keeping an honest man from his bed. I'll charge you overtime.' He nodded at Dan. 'Who's this then, Jim? More slave labour?'

'My nephew, Dan,' said Jim. 'Dan, Mr Hawtrey, who calls himself a vet!'

But even while they joked Dan noticed that Mr Hawtrey wasted no time. He had changed his jacket for an overall and had his sleeves rolled high before Jim had finished speaking, and when he went into the heifer's pen his movements were slow and his voice was quiet.

He examined her carefully, running a gentle hand down her neck before he felt her distended sides and looked at her swollen vulva.

'How long has she been like this?' he asked at last.

'I'm not sure,' said Jim. 'I found her soon after nine. She isn't due to calve just yet and I forgot to check her. I brought her straight down from the field as soon as I realized. She's ready to drop the calf but there's no sign of it. Sorry, Tony. I should have called you earlier.'

'Not to worry,' Tony Hawtrey's voice was reassuring. 'We'll soon sort her out.'

Fascinated, Dan watched as the vet smeared grease on his hands and arms, and then, pushing the heifer's tail to one side, slipped his right hand with a slow twisting movement through the distended opening in her vulva. His hand disappeared and his forearm. His eyes shut as he centred all his concentration on his fingers seeking for the calf, searching for what was wrong, bracing himself as her contracting muscles tightened on his own.

'There's the head,' he said. 'So it's the right way round. And there's a hoof.' He paused and then shook his head. 'Can't find the other,' he said at last. 'Must be tucked underneath. That's where your trouble is. I'll try and shift it, Jim. Wait until she's had her next contraction and then hold her still.'

They waited in silence. The contraction came and passed. Jim held the heifer's head, soothing her with his voice. There was sweat on the vet's forehead and his shoulder muscles were tense with the effort of his hidden hand.

The heifer lowed in sudden distress, and her head jerked as she tried to move.

'Hold her!' the vet said sharply, and then let his breath go on a long sigh of relief. Slowly he freed himself and stepped back. The sweat was running into his eyes. He wiped it away with his clean hand and looked ruefully at the other. It was covered with mucus and blood and there was blood on the front of his overall.

'She's got muscles like a boa-constrictor. I'll be black and blue tomorrow!' he complained, but he was smiling and his voice was cheerful. 'I've straightened the little blighter out. Let's see if she can do the rest herself.'

One contraction and then another came and passed. Behind him the grown-ups were talking quietly but Dan stood watching, willing the tired beast to go on pushing, willing the calf to be born. But nothing happened.

'What do you think, Tony?' That was Uncle Jim.

And the vet answering, 'Give her a bit longer. I could try and pull it out but I might damage her. It's worth waiting. I don't want to operate unless I have to.'

And Auntie Pat, 'I'll go back to the house and get things ready just in case. Call me if you want me.'

'Please,' begged Dan silently. 'Please try a bit harder. I know you're tired and it hurts, but please try.'

Her feet were straddled wide. Her eyes had lost all their brightness and she was shivering.

'She's going to die,' thought Dan as another contraction shook her; and then,

'Uncle Jim, look,' he cried, and his voice cracked with excitement. He could see hooves. They were pale, almost transparent, but unmistakably two hooves.

'Thank God,' said Jim and slipped back into the pen.

'That's my girl,' he soothed her. 'Come on now, you're nearly there. That's my girl.'

Now Dan could see the calf's forelegs, slender and incredibly delicate. The vet held them firmly, pulling gently with each contraction, helping the heifer's tired muscles do their work. Dan leant forward gripping the side of the pen, holding his breath. He watched with incredulous wonder as the calf's legs grew inch by inch, as its muzzle appeared and then its domed forehead and round flattened ears. For a moment head and legs hung there; then Mr Hawtrey stepped back and slowly, easily now, the body followed the head, and the calf slithered gently down its mother's back legs, to lie in a crumpled heap on the straw.

The heifer turned sharply, startled by the strange thing she had felt. She saw the calf and poked it roughly with her nose but it lay still except for the quick rise and fall of its breathing. She poked at it again, and backed away, head lowered as though it was an enemy. It still did not move. Curiosity overcame her fear. Cautiously she came towards it and sniffed hard at its damp coat. She sniffed again, and then instinctively, comfortingly, she began to lick it. Her warm tongue curling round its head, cleaning the mucus from its eyes and ears, claiming it as her own. And its head lifted; its eyes opened, dark and beautiful; it stirred in the straw, moving its long spreadeagled legs. It was alive. It was perfect.

Dan drew a long shaky breath and discovered to his astonishment that he was crying. The tears were pouring down his cheeks, and he did not mind at all. Uncle Jim was smiling broadly, reaching out a grimy hand to grip the vet's even dirtier one, and the vet was smiling too.

Dan gulped, sniffed and grinned back at them.

'I'll go and tell Auntie Pat,' he said, and ran quickly out into the dark yard.

Chapter 15

THE CALF was a heifer. She looked as though she would grow into as good a beast as her mother, and Uncle Jim was delighted with her. Bull calves were sold early to be reared elsewhere for the fat stock market because Uncle Jim had no spare grazing. But a heifer calf was valuable and Dan was overjoyed that this particular one would stay on the farm and eventually join the herd.

Dan looked after her, teaching her to drink from a bucket by dipping his fingers in the milk and giving them to her to suck, gradually getting her nose closer and closer to the pail until she could drink the milk herself. At first she blew and spluttered and choked, but patience and hunger eventually won and soon she was rushing to the door with the other calves whenever she heard the buckets clattering in the dairy.

Dan had regularly fed all of them since he came to the farm, but this one was special. He had watched her being born. When she pushed against him, butting the bucket so fiercely that it was hard to hold it steady and the milk slopped on to his boots, it seemed incredible that this was the same lifeless little creature he had seen lying in the straw, its ribs arching painfully with its first breath. Every time he saw her he remembered that night, and he would slip into the shed whenever he could, just to take a quick look at her and make sure she was all right. He was proud of her. She was *his* calf.

The hay was in at last, and the big dutch barn was

packed tight with bales right up to the roof. Everyone relaxed. The routine work seemed easy now the extra pressure of haymaking was over. There was time to spare. George had a day off to take his wife shopping in town and Auntie Pat went with them, looking incredibly smart in a skirt and high-heeled shoes; and one afternoon Uncle Jim slipped down to the cottage with Dan. He was rather guilty about it, which amused Dan, but it did not stop him from staying to share a pot of tea with Mr 'Uggett.

He admired the garden, inspected Ferret with genuine approval, and, poker-faced, suggested another bit of 'hedging' they might like to get on with when they had time.

The feeling of unhurried freedom was infectious. Lulled by it Dan wandered happily through the days, and the letter from home when at last it came took him completely by surprise.

It arrived as usual on a Tuesday morning. When he came in at lunch-time he saw it propped on the dresser. But when he went to get it his Aunt stopped him.

'Dan,' she said, and something in her voice made him turn and look at her.

She was deliberately matter of fact.

'I had a letter too,' she said, trying to smile. 'Your mother and father have managed to book that holiday they promised you all. School ends in a week. They're going to come and fetch you on the last day of term and then you'll all have some time together to get ready for the holiday. A cottage in Cornwall,' she added brightly. 'That sounds fun.'

'Yes,' said Dan politely. He took the letter from the dresser and put it, unopened, into his pocket.

He was very quiet during lunch. If they spoke to him directly he answered them but he did not look at them,

and when he had finished his first course he put his knife and fork neatly together and said carefully,

'I don't think I want any pudding, thank you, Auntie Pat. Do you mind if I go out now?'

'No, of course not,' she said, trying to pretend there was nothing unusual in his lack of appetite. 'Take an apple in case you feel hungry later.'

'Thank you,' he said and took one. But it was only to please her.

As the door shut behind him she looked with despair at Jim, but before she could speak he put out a hand and gripped her arm hard.

'Don't say it, love,' he said. 'This isn't his home. He's got to go. So don't say it.'

She nodded, staring at the table, then got abruptly to her feet and packed the plates together as though she hated them.

Outside the sun was unsympathetically bright. Dan walked quickly across the yard to the far side of the dutch barn where he was hidden from the kitchen window. The bales of hay were warm against his back and when he moved his shoulders little specks of dust floated down on to his boots. He stared blankly across the drying green at the apple tree. Its leaves were dark green and the clusters of small hard apples showed pale against them. He still had not climbed the tree. He never would now. A week, only a week. He would not be here when the apples were ripe.

He pushed himself fiercely away from the wall of hay and ran headlong across the field. He had to get away. He did not want to see anybody, not even Mr 'Uggett. He hated them all.

It was not fair! Why didn't Auntie Pat ask him to stay? Why should his parents make him go back? What gave them the right to tell him what to do? Mr 'Uggett said it was because they loved him. Well, too bad! He'd show them when he got home.

He stopped running. He was panting and unbearably hot. His feet hurt inside his gumboots and the hair on his forehead was wet. He was overwhelmed by the sense of his helplessness. There was nothing, absolutely nothing that he could do. If he were grown up he would be able to choose for himself. But he wasn't. He had to do what he was told. There was nowhere to run to, no way out. He wouldn't see the corn cut, he wouldn't eat the parsnips he had planted in Mr 'Uggett's garden. In a week he would say goodbye to them all, leave the farm, leave Ferret.

'I can't do it,' he said desperately. 'I won't.' But he knew it was no use.

He walked all afternoon, so miserable that any unhappiness he had ever felt before seemed like nothing. He did not want to think about anything, and walked blindly, trying to find something to comfort him, but wherever he walked in the woods Dog and Ben went beside him; and the hedgerows were full of the burrows where Ferret had hunted. Each place had its memories and he said goodbye

to each one. His misery engulfed him until he was aware
of nothing else.

An unfamiliar sound, sudden as the crack of a twig,
brought him at last to a halt. Puzzled, he looked round.
He was quite close to the farm, beside the dew
pond where he had dumped the stranded tadpoles, and
the field was empty. But something must have made that
noise.

He stood still for a moment wondering what it was, but
he did not really care. His left heel was throbbing, he
thought he must have blistered it, and the water in the
pond looked cool. He kicked off his gumboots, obscurely
pleased to find that his heel was bleeding and raw, and
started to roll up his jeans. What a pity, he thought, that
he could swim so well; and his mind toyed with the
dramatic picture of his lifeless body found floating among
the waterweed. That would show them!

The second crack really startled him. It came from close
behind him and he spun round, searching the hedge for
movement. All he saw was the bird.

It broke from the hedge, its wings beating frantically as
it tried to gain height. It made a few yards and then
faltered, spiralling slowly downwards to fall with a thud at

Dan's feet. Horrified he bent and picked it up. It was a cock chaffinch.

He felt its heart race against his hand for one brief moment, and then it stopped, the lids closed over its eyes and it was still. The rose pink feathers of its breast were torn and stained and there was blood on his fingers. It was dead. It had been shot. He stood quite still, cradling it in his hands, not a bird any more, just a fragile bundle of bones and feathers. Dead.

He was still holding it when a boy pushed his way through a gap further down the hedge, saw Dan and strolled towards him. Tucked under one arm was a gun.

''Allo,' he said cheerfully. 'You twagging it too?'

'Twagging it?' Dan was surprised to find his voice so steady and expressionless.

'From school,' explained the boy. He flicked a careless finger at the chaffinch.

'I got it then. I thought I had.'

'Oh yes,' said Dan. 'You got it.'

He turned away and carefully laid the bird on the grass beside his gumboots. Then he stood up and stared at the boy. He seemed to see him with extraordinary clarity. He was a big boy, taller and heavier than Dan with a broad freckled face and dark hair. A button was missing from his shirt and his leather boots were dusty. The fingernails of the hand holding the gun were broken and dirty and when he shifted his grip the gun barrel gleamed grey in the sunlight. The shell of misery that had wrapped Dan all afternoon splintered into rage.

'Get off my land,' he said fiercely. 'Give me that gun and get out!'

The boy's eyes widened with surprise and his hands tightened on the gun, holding it close to his chest.

'Like hell I will!' he jeered. 'You want it, you come and get it.'

Dan took a deep breath and charged. Instinctively he went in low and he was lucky. His head caught the other boy squarely in the stomach and he staggered back gasping. Dan tore the gun out of his slack hands and without stopping to think whether it was loaded threw it as hard as he could towards the pond. He did not have time to see if it had fallen in the water. His momentary advantage was gone and the boy was on him.

He lost count of time. He just fought. Fists thudded into his body and bruised his face, but his own knuckles were sore and the boy's nose was bleeding. A stone cut his bare feet and he slipped and fell but he grabbed at the boy's shirt and brought him down too; and then they were both rolling over and over on the ground kicking and pummelling at each other in a cloud of dust.

Neither of them heard the tractor or George's voice shouting at them. It was not until he heaved them roughly to their feet, holding them apart at arm's length, that they realized that he was there.

'That's enough!' he said and shook them before he let them go. 'What the blazes is going on?'

The boys stood and glowered at him, gasping for breath. Then they both spoke at once.

'He took my gun!'

'He shot a chaffinch!'

'A gun? Where is it?'

Dan pointed. It was lying by the edge of the pool, the stock just clear of the water. George picked it up and looked at it.

'That's mine,' the boy muttered.

'I see.' Thoughtfully George weighed it in his hand and then, making up his mind, tucked it under his arm.

'Now look here, Billy Owen,' he said sternly, 'you've no right on this land and you know it. And you've no right shooting birds. It's against the law. So you get off home.

Fast. And as for the gun, well, I reckon I'll hang on to it for now. I'll bring it back this evening when your Dad's home.'

Billy opened his mouth to protest but George was too angry for argument.

'Get off with you!' he said, and Billy plunged through the hedge and was gone.

'Young varmint!' said George. 'His Dad's a friend of mine. He'll deal with him.' He grinned at Dan. 'You were really duffing him, weren't you? Maybe I should have left it to you.'

Still chuckling he climbed on to the tractor and started the engine.

'You all right then?' he shouted above the noise. 'I could turn round and take you back to the yard if you like.'

Dan shook his head.

'I'm all right,' he said.

He watched George drive away and then, his legs suddenly shaky, sat down quickly on the grass. Tenderly he explored the damage to his face. His cheek was swollen and his lips felt stiff and he rather thought he would have a black eye by the evening as well as a cut foot and a mass of bruises, but he was all right. He felt fine. It was as though all his unhappiness had exploded into the fight and disappeared.

Something was digging into a bruise on his leg. He pushed his hand into the pocket of his trousers and pulled out the apple he had taken from the kitchen. It was very battered. He spat the brown bits out and ate the rest. The juice stung his lip but it tasted sharp and cleaned the dust out of his mouth.

He washed his face in the pond, gingerly at first and then vigorously, dunking his head again and again into the cold water until his hair dripped on to his shirt collar; and then he paddled round the edge, kicking the water up in fountains

until his jeans were as wet as his shirt. Then he buried the chaffinch carefully, and lay down in the sun to dry.

At last he read his parents' letter. It was all there, just as Auntie Pat had told him, except for one thing.

'It will be lovely to have you back,' his mother had written. 'We have missed you so. It's been a long time.'

Perhaps it would not be so bad at home; anyway he had got to go so he might as well make the best of it. And there was a whole week left. You could do a lot in a week if you did not waste time.

He looked terrible when he got back to the farm. His clothes were caked with mud and dust and his cheek had started bleeding again. Auntie Pat was horrified but Jim told her not to fuss and whipped him off to the bathroom to clean him up. Dan went with him gratefully. He was aching all over, his story was told and he was tired right down to his bones. Uncle Jim might be heavy handed with the disinfectant, but he was very understanding.

'Can I come back, Uncle Jim?' he asked suddenly.

Jim stopped dabbing at his face and looked at him, obviously surprised.

'Of course you can. Whenever you like.'

'When I'm grown up? Can I come then?'

Jim bent over him with a fresh piece of cotton wool. Dan could not see his face.

'You'll need a job when you've grown up,' he said.

'I know,' said Dan. 'That's what I meant.'

'I see.' Carefully Jim measured Elastoplast and cut it to size. 'My family,' he said thoughtfully, 'have worked this land for over a hundred years. I'd like it to stay that way.'

'But am I family?' asked Dan.

'Oh yes,' said Jim. 'You're family all right,' and stuck the plaster firmly across his cheek.

'Feeling better now?' said Auntie Pat, when they came downstairs.

Dan's lips were stiff and it hurt to smile, but he managed it.

'Don't worry,' he said cheerfully. 'I'm fine now.'

But only he and Uncle Jim knew that he was not talking about his bruises.

Chapter 16

THE DAYS flew by. Dan tried very hard just to enjoy them and not to think ahead. He wore his black eye like a badge of honour. Mr 'Uggett had roared with laughter when he had first seen it, but when he had heard the whole story he had nodded solemnly and said,

'You'll be all right now then, won't you? He's a big lad, Billy Owen. You did well to stand up to him and have nothing worse than a black eye at the end of it. I reckon you could cope with anyone now!'

One morning near the end of the week Mr 'Uggett called at Willowgarth. He chose his time deliberately, knowing that Dan had gone to market with Jim to sell some pigs. Dan had told him all about it, excited at the prospect of his first market day.

'Isn't it lucky the pigs were ready?' he had said. 'I did want to see the market before I went home and I thought I wouldn't be able to. Of course I could have gone just to look round, but it's different when you've got stock to sell.'

Mr 'Uggett had agreed and made a silent note of the day. That would suit his plans very well.

Pat was surprised to see him but knew better than to show it. She stopped work and made tea, carefully choosing matching cups and saucers. A formal visit from Ben 'Uggett was an occasion and the old family mugs just would not do!

Ben sat quietly at the end of the table, his hat balanced on his knee, and took his time. They discussed the weather,

and the state of the farm; inquired after each other's health and exchanged news about the village. It was Pat who first mentioned Dan.

'Ah,' said Ben. 'I wanted to ask you summat about Dan.'

'Yes?' said Pat encouragingly.

'Well, it's like this, see,' Ben leant forward. 'I didn't want to speak to Dan till I'd seen you, in case you had plans of your own. But there's something I'd like to show him before he goes home. It'd mean staying out a bit late, like, but I thought he could have a bit of supper with me, and I'd see him back here after. That is if you're agreeable?'

'Of course I am, Mr Huggett,' said Pat warmly, touched that he should have bothered to consult her. 'Which evening were you thinking of?'

'Whichever suits.'

Pat thought for a moment.

'If it's something really special,' she said at last, 'what about Monday? He goes home on Tuesday morning so it would be his last evening here. I think he'd like to spend it with you.'

A smile of real pleasure spread across Ben's face.

'That'd be grand,' he said, 'if it's all right by you. We'll say Monday then?'

'Yes,' said Pat. 'We'll say Monday.'

When Ben told him, Dan was thrilled. A whole evening with Mr 'Uggett, supper at the cottage and time to play with Ferret and Dog without having to rush back for the milking. And Mr 'Uggett had something special to show him.

'Well,' said Ben slowly. 'Struck me the other day as there's one thing you've never seen. So I thought we'd try our luck. I thought we'd go and watch for badgers.'

Badgers! Dan was speechless. He knew a lot about badgers because Ben had told him. The tracks which they followed through the woods and fields were made by the badgers; secret, hidden paths which tunnelled through thickets and tall bracken, trodden out by years of use. He had found the sets where they lived, and occasionally seen a footprint in the wet earth, unmistakable with its long curved claws, or picked a tuft of stiff grey and white hairs from a barbed wire fence.

The sets, Ben told him, had been used for hundreds of years; generation after generation of badgers adding to the piles of excavated earth, treading down the open space round about and using the same paths night after night. Old Brock, people called the badger, the Old Man, the Wise One of the Woods, and a wisp of his hair wrapped round your finger would keep you safe and guard you against the Evil Eye. Because he saw the signs of their presence and never saw them, because they were so elusive and shy, badgers to Dan were more than just special. Badgers were magic.

He prayed for a fine evening. Rain would be disastrous. He prayed for a light but steady breeze to carry their scent away from the set. Ben warned him they might wait for hours and see nothing, but he knew that would not happen. On Tuesday morning he would have to go away; but on Monday night he would see the badgers.

The last few days were very strange. Dan felt as though he were drifting and did not belong anywhere. He carried round with him like a weight the sadness of all his goodbyes, and longed for the time to pass quickly so that he could say them and be gone. Waiting to leave was worse than leaving.

Monday would have been unbearable if he had not had the evening to look forward to. He clung to the thought of it like a climber to a precarious fingerhold. Everyone was very kind and tried to make sure that he was kept busy. He was grateful but it did not really help, and by the end of the day he was near to tears. He needed Ben 'Uggett, for Ben was always the same.

Dog met him at the gate as usual and led him gaily through the garden to the back door. Ben took one look at his white tense face, got up from his chair and went to the stove. Food was what was needed, he decided.

'There's a cloth in the left-hand drawer, and knives and forks in the right,' he said. 'Set the table for me, Dan, then we can eat and be off.'

There was hot boiled bacon and piles of new potatoes; hunks of buttered bread and cheese and raspberries from the garden. Warmed and comforted, Dan relaxed.

They lingered over their mugs of tea, talking quietly. It was important, Ben explained, to arrive at the set at just the right time, well before the badgers were likely to emerge, so their scent would have drifted away and the birds would have accepted their presence. They washed up the dishes and tidied the kitchen and then at last Ben went to the back door and looked out.

'Get your jacket on, Dan,' he said. 'It's time to go.'

They went along the lane and up through the beech woods. The sun was setting and the light came slantwise through the trunks, golden and still. They walked carefully, changing direction to keep the light breeze constantly towards them, moving always deeper into the wood.

Ben stopped at last on the edge of a small clearing and beckoned Dan to come close.

'There,' he said, and pointed. 'It's across there, through those elder bushes. Now listen, Dan. Once we're settled, don't talk and keep still. If them badgers hear you moving they'll stay down till they know you've gone. Some nights I've waited hours and never seen a hair of 'em.'

'I'll be careful,' said Dan. 'I'm very good at keeping still. I've been well trained!'

From where they stood the bushes looked impenetrable but when they got closer Dan saw they were only a screen. Slowly they edged through them and there in a small bank under the protecting branches of a yew tree was the badger set.

They sat on the ground with their backs against the twisted elder trunk and waited. A low branch helped to hide them, but still left space for them to see and the breeze which moved the leaves blew softly on their faces. The light was fading rapidly, and as the overall stillness grew Dan became aware of a myriad of small sounds.

A minute russet wren dipped from branch to branch above their heads searching for insects in the bark. Close by something rustled suddenly among the dead leaves and then was still, and he could hear the high thready squeaking of a mouse. High above them in the beech wood a bird began to sing. Beautiful, unexpected, the notes floated down to them in the dusk and Dan listened entranced. It was too late for a blackbird or a thrush. This was a nightingale.

Whether he had closed his eyes to listen or whether his sight had blurred with the strain of staring at the set he never knew; but suddenly, as though the nightingale's song had been a signal, there was the badger.

It stood like a grey rock at the entrance to the set, its heavy body quite still, its striped head turned towards them. A shudder of fear went through Dan. In the half light it seemed so big and strange; a mythical beast, not bone and blood.

It seemed to be looking straight at them and Dan held his breath in case it had sensed their presence. But it turned, lifting its head as it tested the wind for any scent of danger, and then padded slowly away up the steep slope into the shadow of the trees.

The warning pressure of Ben's hand kept Dan from moving and at the same time he heard a most extraordinary noise, a muffled squeaking and squealing under the earth. Deep inside the set something was happening.

The noise stopped and once more they waited. Then something stirred in the dark entrance and slowly a second badger appeared. It was smaller than the first and more cautious. It stood quite still for a long time making sure that all was safe before it moved to one side, grunting deep in its throat. And tumbling from the set in answer to that call, to Dan's astonished delight came two cubs.

They still had their fluffy baby fur and their long noses were an absurd contrast to their round bodies. They squeaked and grunted like young piglets, butting at the sow badger, climbing on to the grey bulk of her body and falling off again. She pinned each one with a heavy forepaw and groomed them in turn, nibbling through the fur on their backs like a bitch with her puppies, and then pushing them away to play.

They fought with each other, rolling over and over in the dead leaves, and chased each other round the little clearing and in and out of the set. They climbed to the top of the steep bank and slid down on their fat bottoms, squealing with excitement and looking so comical that Dan had to bite his lip to stop himself laughing.

At last the inevitable happened, and one of them missed his footing and cannoned into the sow with a thud. She had been resting peacefully and resented the disturbance. The cub had gone too far and needed to be taught a lesson. She rose with a grunt and swiped at him with her paw. She knocked him backwards, and he somersaulted across the open space to land in a tumbled heap against Dan's feet. It startled them both. In spite of himself Dan moved. The cub lay petrified, staring up at him with bright brown eyes; then it shrilled a high warning and ran for the safety of the set. Within seconds the badgers had gone.

Ben sighed and rose stiffly to his feet, stretching his arms to get the cramp out of them. Then he reached a hand down to Dan.

'Time to go home,' he said softly. 'They won't come again tonight.'

The darkness closed round them as they walked back down the hill. Dan stumbled and shivered, suddenly cold, and grateful for Ben's guiding hand on his shoulder. The badgers and the nightingale seemed like a dream and it was hard to come back to reality.

All too soon they reached the farm. Ben stopped at the gate and Dan turned to look at him. The faint starlight left his face in shadow, but Dan knew he was smiling and when he spoke his voice was quiet and comforting.

'Dan,' he said. 'There's some folk you say goodbye to and some where there's no need. You'll be back, Dan; I know you'll be back.'

'Oh, Mr 'Uggett,' said Dan, and his voice choked in his throat.

Ben's hands were hard on his shoulders.

'Listen, Dan,' he said. 'Things don't change because you leave them. The woods and the farm and the land will still be here. And the people. We'll all be waiting for you.'

'And Ferret? You'll take care of Ferret?'

'I'll keep him safe for you.'

Ben held out his hand and Dan put his into it, gripped it tight and felt the answering pressure of Ben's rough fingers.

'Goodnight, Dan,' said Ben.

Dan struggled with his voice and won.

'Goodnight, Mr 'Uggett,' he said. And then he was standing alone by the gate watching Mr 'Uggett walking away.

Half-way up the lane he stopped and turned.

'Dan,' he called. 'Remember tonight!'

Dan stared into the darkness, straining to catch the last glimpse of him, but he had gone, disappearing as silently as he had done at their first meeting. He had gone. It was over. This was the end of his last evening.

And then suddenly Dan knew what Mr 'Uggett had meant. This was his last evening but it had brought him his first nightingale, his first badgers. He must and he would remember tonight, for it was Ben's way of making him understand that this was not the end but the beginning.